JN105520

Giving Back One-Hundred-Fold

人生の百倍返し

Volume 3

Departure
To the Distant World

遠い世界へ

YAMAGUCHI Katsumi

Translation & Localization
Harley Emmons

文芸社

The Story So Far

Naoto Yamamoto, who joined the Marunouchi Bank in 1976, acquired his accounting knowledge at his first branch, the Fukuoka branch, which became a weapon for his subsequent work. Mr. Sugayama, the president of a close business partner, taught him about the 'site-first principle'. After working in two sales positions, he was transferred to the planning department, where he served eight bank presidents and remained for a quarter of a century. During that time, Naoto was a liaison for the Ministry of Finance (MOF), and continued that position for a long time. After that, he was also involved in listing Marunouchi Bank on the New York Stock Exchange, and used this experience to confront the problem of non-performing loans caused by the bursting of the bubble economy in Japan. He fought against the government's old-fashioned 'do nothing' policy towards banks.

However, he was forced to resign due to a tax problem associated with the rescue merger of UBJ Bank–a merger by Mitsuwa Bank and Toyo Bank. Naoto looked back on his thirty-five years as a banker, where he was immersed in his work with no time to care for his family. He thanked whoever would listen again for the life and family he had been given.

Even at the accounting education foundation, which became his second workplace, he managed to avoid the dissolution of the program, and after that he devoted himself to training practical accounting students after they passed the certified public accountant examination. Meanwhile, in order to attract foreign investments, the Japanese government launched a national project to have Japanese companies introduce international accounting standards, and ordered Naoto to lead the project. Although he struggled in the position, he was steadily producing results.

However, Yoko began developing symptoms. In order to help Yoko recover completely, Naoto quit the foundation halfway through and devoted himself to taking care of his wife who had taken care of him for decades. At that time, Takeshi Terada, a student of his who admired Naoto and joined Marunouchi UBJ Bank, died in an accident due to fatigue and overwork. Naoto was enraged at the lack of attendance at the young man's funeral. Naoto then realized that it was thanks to the many corporate warriors who sacrificed themselves for the sake of the bank that allowed it to prosper.

While taking care of Yoko, Naoto renewed his determination to dedicate the rest of his life to the orphaned children of those corporate warriors and children who, like Yoko, were also battling intractable diseases. As Naoto devoted himself to taking care of Yoko at home, he also began to think about their families.

One day, Kumi, the eldest daughter who took in their

dog Great in Zushi, called to say, "This morning, Great was summoned to heaven, passing away while sleeping on my lap."

Great must have come to say goodbye to her longtime owner, Yoko. At that time, Yoko, who was sick and unable to speak, managed to call out, "Great, Great," as if the dog was right next to her. It was undoubtedly the beloved dog Great's repayment to her family.

After that, Naoto learned that his old bank, which had reached the top rank, had lost its next goal, and that the educational foundation had lost sight of its original purpose. He had to intervene and pay back the people who he owed his career to. In the meantime, Yoko's intractable disease gradually progressed, and she no longer knew who her husband, Naoto, was. Furthermore, at the same time, Naoto's mother, who had been living in Kawasaki, passed away. The following year, his mother-in-law, who had single-handedly supported Yoko's family for many years, passed away too.

However, his sister-in-law and brother-in-law didn't care about Yoko's condition and they started a bloody battle over his mother-in-law's inheritance. Naoto asked himself, "What is the most important thing for human beings to live?" while continuing daily home care. Meanwhile, he received news that Hiratsuka, who joined Marunouchi Bank in the same year as him, also had an incurable disease. The man was suddenly confined to a wheelchair, but he nevertheless lived positively with the devoted support of his wife. Naoto learned the true 'joy and sorrow of life' in their marital love.

Giving Back One-Hundred-Fold Volume3
Departure To the Distant World

CONTENTS

Part 3 Nostalgia

Main Characters

Part 1 Bank Edition

· Yamamoto, Naoto – Marunouchi Bank Fukuoka and Motosumiyoshi Branch Employee, Investigator/Deputy Chief in the Planning Division,Tsukishima Branch Deputy Manager

· Ogi, Hiroaki – Marunouchi Bank Fukuoka Branch Employee (same orientation class as Naoto)

· Yamanouchi, Katsundo – Marunouchi Bank Fukuoka Branch Managing Director

· Shimazaki, Eikichi – Marunouchi Bank Fukuoka Branch Deputy Manager

· Tanahashi, Kenichi – Marunouchi Bank Fukuoka Branch Chief of Foreign Exchange Loan Division, San Francisco Branch office Manager

· Kouda, Osamu – Marunouchi Bank Fukuoka Branch Employee (Naoto's junior)

· Ayanokouji, Kaoru – Marunouchi Corporation Fukuoka Branch Employee (Naoto's childhood friend)

· Tomita, Jiro – Hakata Police station Assistant Director

· Matsubara, Shuuichi – Marunouchi Bank Tsukishima Branch Managing Director

· Hasebe, Tadashi – Marunouchi Bank Tsukishima Branch Sales Manager

· Tanabe, Hiroshi – Mitsuwa Bank Tsukishima Branch Managing Director, Mitsuwa Bank President

· Murata, Hideo – Ministry of Justice Civil Affairs Division Assistant Manager

· Takeda, Takezou – Cabinet Office Minister for Finance

· Osaki, Shunichi – Ministry of Finance Bank Department Manager, Inspection Department Manager

· Hirata, Makoto – Marunouchi Bank Motosumiyoshi Branch Employee (Naoto's Junior)

Part 2 Nursing Edition
- Yamamoto, Naoto – Retiree (At-Home Caregiver)
- Yamamoto, Yoko – Naoto's Wife (Registered Nurse)
- Ueki, Kinichi – Deputy Director of Nagasaki Roadside Psychiatric Hospital
- Asai, Jiro – Nagasaki Tozai Hospital Neurologist
- Sugiyama, Saburo – Sakuradamon Hospital Neurologist
- Kyoko, Honma – Sakuradamon Hospital Physician

Part 3 Nostalgia Edition
- Yamamoto, Naoto – Retiree (At-Home Caregiver)
- Yamamoto, Yoko – Naoto's Wife (Registered Nurse)
- Yamamoto, Kumi – Naoto's Daughter
- Yamamoto, Aiko – Naoto's Mother
- Yamamoto, Masao – Naoto's Father
- Tomiyama, Saburo – Retiree (Naoto's childhood friend)
- Ouno, Fujiko – Daionji Kindergarten teacher (Ouno obstetrics and gynecology hospital Director's wife)
- Kuroiwa, Eiko – Minami Oura primary school teacher
- Arie, Shinnosuke – Umegasaki junior high school basket club captain (Naoto's classmate)
- Yamashita, Suma – Yoko's mother
- Yamashita, Kumi – Yoko's sister
- Yamashita, Yuu – Yoko's brother
- Mutou, Kayo – Yoko's sister
- Mutou, Ikuji – Kayo's husband

Part 1
Bank Edition

Prologue Bachelor's Pad

November 22, 2019, Naoto started Yoko's at-home nursing in Nagasaki. At first, he was completely engrossed in their day-to-day life because it was the first of this kind experience in their lives. However, around this time, the novel coronavirus began to spread like wildfire and the government restricted people leaving their homes to only once to the grocery store every three days. One day on the way to the supermarket, he ran into a group of young faces in brand-new suits gathered around Miyazakidai Station on the Tokyu Den-en-toshi Line– obviously new employees. The scene stops Naoto in his tracks and sends him right back to when he started his career.

If you ask a salaried worker, "What was the best time of your career?", most people would answer their first few years. Naoto joined the former Marunouchi Bank on April 1, 1976, and was first assigned to the Fukuoka branch for his first year of training as a working adult. The Fukuoka branch was the main executive branch in the Kyushu area, with three other branch offices in Kitakyushu, Nagasaki, and Kumamoto. More than 150 employees were enrolled there, three times more than the present-day amount. During the office-wide trip held every fall, it was customary to charter three large buses and visit sightseeing spots all over Kyushu.

Like the main store, the Fukuoka branch building had an atrium in the middle, and was made of marble, giving it a solid, dignified atmosphere. On the first floor, there was the branch manager's seat in the center, with two deputy branch managers' seats below it, and the sales section, funds section, and loan and foreign exchange section were arranged to surround the three main offices. In addition, there was a general affairs office next to the staff entrance on the first floor. On the second floor was the external affairs department, on the third floor was a meeting room, library, and a 'telephone switchboard', a technology now lost to the ages. The fourth floor was the staff cafeteria and lounge.

Six newcomers, three men and three women, were assigned to the Fukuoka branch that year. The men were Hiroaki Ogi, a graduate of Kyoto University, Naoto, a graduate of Nagasaki University, and Koji Morishita, a graduate of Kumamoto Commercial High School. The women were Tomoko Amano, Yoshiko Suenaga, and Seika Sato, all of whom had just graduated from a local high school. Naoto was assigned to the section that handled ordinary deposits and commercial accounts. Ogi was assigned to the foreign exchange section, which handled domestic remittances and dividend payments, and Morishita was assigned as a cashier who handled cash and checks. In the women's group, Amano was assigned to the time deposit clerk, Suenaga was assigned to the telephone switchboard, and Sato was assigned to deal with funds and capital.

The six newcomers were always the first to be nominated for extracurriculars, and were forced to provide the entertainment at company events. The annual welcome party for new employees was held at Ohori Park with the cherry blossoms in full bloom. The newbies had been ordered to stake out a prime spot–thinking back, it was the last peaceful moment before the approaching storm. At that time, the custom at cherry blossom viewing parties was 'The Electric Wire' song and dance. The lyrics about a hunter and three sparrows up on the telephone wires fluttered in the air along with the cheers, dance moves, and petals. In addition, Pink Lady's songs 'UFO' and 'Pepper Inspector' were explosively popular for everyone to sing along to.

The dormitory for single men was located right next to the coast of Momochi in Nishijin, Nishi Ward (now Sawara Ward), Fukuoka City. The building was two stories, with the dining room, bathroom, and manager's office on the first floor, and eight studio apartments on the second floor. The innermost room was the manager's personal room, and the only one equipped with air conditioning. The dormitory manager at that time was Kenichi Tanahashi, who joined the company in 1970, and spent every Sunday training Naoto and Ogi in the basics of being a banker. Tanahashi was second-in-command to the then Ministry of International Trade and Industry (now the Ministry of Economy, Trade and Industry) for two years before being transferred to the Fukuoka branch. After work, he liked to take the new recruits to a pub called "Maki" by the Jigyo River near the bachelors' dorms. The proprietress was a genuine Hakata native with a frank, refreshing personality.

This izakaya bar became the hangout for all the young employees from Marunouchi Bank and New Japan Industrial Bank to engage in rowdy debates about the state of the world.

"Loaning money is the lifeblood of the economy," Tanahashi would say. He had developed his theory that the role of private banks would become increasingly important for Japanese companies to grow in the future, and the employees of New Japan Industrial Bank emphasized the importance of conducting corporate surveys. Both Naoto and Ogi listened with stars in their eyes.

After that, Tanahashi transferred to the Information Development section at the head office (a department that matched the needs of business partners between branches, mainly in overseas fields). Naoto, who was transferred to the planning department, would meet him again in San Francisco more than ten years later. At that time, Japanese banks were scrambling to raise capital in order to meet the international capital adequacy regulations pledged by banks around the world. In order to attract a large amount of investment not only from domestic institutional investors, but also from overseas ones, companies frequently held information sessions (public relations activities) around the world to solicit investments.

Naoto had traveled abroad repeatedly to accompany his old manager, the newly-appointed Deputy President Kenichi Tanahashi. As the director of the San Francisco office at the time, it was Naoto's duty to pick up Tanahashi at the airport.

"Mr. Tanahashi, it's been a while," Naoto greeted, getting out to open the other car door. "I never thought we'd be meeting up on the other side of the globe."

"It has. I see you've moved up in the world too. It's an unimaginable career advancement, I remember you were always trying to jump ahead. Your old roommate Ogi also visited San Francisco on a business trip last month. My two proteges, becoming leaders with the future of the company on your shoulders." Tanahashi had a blissful smile on his face the whole ride.

However, Tanahashi's luck took a turn after they parted ways again. The man decided to return to Japan after falling ill. He had overworked himself for years and smoked heavily, unable to give up cigarettes for many years. He had been cornered with "Stage IV" lung cancer.

As soon as Tanahashi returned to Japan, he called up Naoto to hold a 'Fukuoka party' for old-times sake. Naoto gathered about 30 young current employees for the celebration, but unfortunately Tanahashi, the guest of honor, was unable to attend due to his worsening illness. A year later, his life ended prematurely–a genius with an abundance of energy to take care of his juniors and work hard, even if it took a toll on his health. Tanahashi's death marked the long line of Naoto's seniors that would soon lose their lives one by one from overworking.

Tanahashi had enthusiastically mentored Naoto and Ogi every Sunday at the bachelor's dorms. While he could no longer hear the old manager's voice, hoarse from alcohol and cigarettes, it still remained as a vivid memory for Naoto.

"Yamamoto, in order to accurately grasp the financial status of our business partners, there are two important things– their current transaction status and their movement of funds. In other words, the 'Summary of Business Partners' and the 'Cash Flows', and you'll have to write these up yourself. When you enter the loan department, try to create a new 'customer summary table' for the companies you're in charge of, so you'll have a deep understanding of the customer all at once. For the 'Cash Flow Chart', consult the person in charge of accounting at each partner business in person–don't only rely on the information your predecessor left.

A company is a living organism, and the flow of funds changes daily. Doing all this yourself should give you a good picture of your customers' current cash flow profile, and, in turn, reveal when your counterparty will need funds. Then, you can be ready to pitch various proposals to said business partners."

Around the bachelors' dorm where Tanahashi had dispensed his wisdom, the Tenjin Underground Shopping Mall was completed to much excitement. But, that left the subway under construction and all employees crammed in trams during rush hour. Naoto and the other newbies had been told they could go home early during their three months of apprenticing, without pulling all-nighters like the rest of the staff. However, after their first big error, Naoto and a few others had to indeed work overtime late into the night

It was an old-fashioned way of working, having so many employees in the sales department work overtime, unable to go home unless they adjusted their calculations. If that kind of overtime pay was racked up every month, then the branch wouldn't turn a profit. But Naoto's doubts were resolved when he submitted the previous month's overtime schedule to his boss. A monthly overtime limit was set for all employees, and no one was expected to exceed that upper target.

Naoto raised the concern with the chief of staff. "Isn't this a violation of the Labor Standards Act?"

"Mr. Yamamoto, this is precisely the strength of Japanese companies."

"Chief, you get paid for all the work you do, don't you? If

not, it'd be a violation of the Labor Standards Act, and you and the other managers will be punished."

"That's the good thing about Japanese companies. You'll understand soon enough."

At that time, there was no such thing as a 'whistleblowing system', and the importance of legal compliance wasn't recognized yet. It was a very convenient time for business owners, and not so much for the employees. Instead, they were forced to work "unpaid overtime" at the end of the financial period. That was considered part of the life of Japanese office workers.

With his first paycheck of 67,000 yen (approximately 670 dollars), Naoto bought himself a large steel desk and chair, and started drinking from the early hours.

"Yamamoto, you have a good sense of etiquette compared to other young men these days," Tanahashi started during their impromptu celebration.

"No, no, it's not like that. I just thought that it would be nice to use my first paycheck to have a drink with the manager who looked out for me when I moved here."

"And that's what makes you stand out from the other newcomers. The rest scatter when they see me coming lately."

Up to this point, things had been going smoothly, so Naoto had no idea that Tanahashi had a reputation for being a heavy drinker. As the dormitory students filed in throughout the night, they would eat at a distance to avoid the two of them. Naoto would ask them to join, but everyone had some sort of vague excuse.

With only the two of them, Tanahashi started up some Kyushu drinking songs. Eventually, another dorm resident chimed in with some of his local folk songs. Soon, they were cajoling Naoto to sing something too. He reluctantly started with the only thing he could remember, a lullaby from his childhood. Thus ended the banquet on the first payday of a new employee.

After that, however, something unexpected happened. It was well after midnight when Deputy Branch Manager Shimazaki, who had been staying in the guest room while on a job away from home, returned in a good mood after a long dinner with a business partner. Considering himself the most important person in the dorms, he immediately woke up the manager and all the residents and ordered them to gather in the dining hall. Sleep-eyed and bed-raggled, everyone hung out in the kitchen–except for Naoto, who had just gotten to bed. Shimazaki took it upon himself to pound on Naoto's door himself the second time.

"You're pretty brave to disobey your direct superiors, newbie. Who the hell do you think you're getting your salary from? You rookies are getting money to sit on your asses and learn from all of us. If you can't listen to what I say, just quit.

You're already fired!"

Naoto finally ran out of patience, shaking off the older man's shouts. "I don't get paid by you. We get paid by our shareholders and business partners, not our bosses. So isn't keeping us up and affecting our performance tomorrow stealing directly from those stakeholders? I'm going back to sleep now."

Shimazaki seemed to have suddenly sobered up at Naoto's words, and scoffed, "Yamamoto, we're bookmarking this for another day."

The other residents grumbled their appreciation and sulked off the bed. However, this was only the beginning of Shimazaki's 'power harassment'. The following incident occurred during a banquet on a trip in the autumn of the following year. Koda Osamu, who was a brand-new employee a year below Naoto, fell prey to the deputy branch manager next.

The regular manager couldn't participate in said trip due to urgent business, so deputy branch manager Shimazaki took charge. At the dinner, the momentum he drank, he revealed his true nature and began to behave arrogantly once again. "Hey, Koda," Shimazaki called across the table, "you're a newcomer, so it's your job to make the party even more lively! You could even dance naked on the table! You salary thief!"

Koda endured the deputy branch manager's power

harassment, but those last words broke his patience. As a student, Koda had been a martial artist of the highest degree and was confident in his physical strength. He approached the deputy manager with a raised fist. Surprised by this, the deputy branch manager threatened him right back.

"Kouda, what's with the fist? Are you going to hit me? If you are, then hurry it up. What are you going to do?"

Naoto jumped up to hold Koda back, drawing Shimazaki's ire even further. "The blind leading the blind? Last year and this year, the newcomers have been increasingly pathetic. Isn't there a rookie with any guts?"

"How much were you able to do when you were a rookie? Did you do a good enough job to match your salary? No one should be able to do that much when they're just starting out. The point is to invest the money in new employees so they can run the future of the company."

"Don't speak like you're a regular employee yet. I don't have any expectations for you guys in the first place. Get out now. You're ruining the taste of the sake."

Naoto and Koda left in a huff, hoping to never directly cross paths with the deputy manager any time soon.

Chapter 1 Love

But of course, the harassment did not stop there. Shimazaki went out of his way to brandish any executive rights he could. At the branch office, all new employees spent their first year in the sales department, and then transferred to another in their second year. Eventually, they would have experience with all of the major departments under their belts after their first four years.

Naoto's roommate, Ogi, transferred to the corporate group under the business division in charge of existing transactions. However, Naoto remained in sales after his first year. Everyone knew the rumor about Naoto getting harassed by the deputy branch manager, even in his dorms. Yet, no one was willing to take the risk of saying it out loud.

One day, Naoto got a call from the Yamanouchi branch manager. "So have you gotten used to the everyday work yet? All of the bank's business starts with collecting deposits. You're working with the building blocks of our operations. It's something you can only study thoroughly as a newcomer. By the way," the manager continued, "I heard your friend Ogi had already been transferred, why haven't you? One of your managers mentioned you wanted to continue in this position, but is that really true? How much more do you think you could learn where you are?"

Naoto wanted to say how it indeed wasn't his choice, but a personal vendetta from a drunk branch manager. Still, it was against his personal code to place the blame on someone else. "Well, I think that the future liberalization of deposit interest rates is going to make the earnings environment for banks even more severe. Specifically, it's needed to unify the clerks on the first floor with the bookkeepers on the second, and reduce costs. So I remained in this position to consult with the chief of staff on a new deposit clerk system."

The partial lie was met with great enthusiasm on the other end of the line. Soon, the Yamanouchi branch manager ran with Naoto's spur of the moment strategy. The feud with Shimazaki had unintentionally landed Naoto as the leader on a new team specifically for cost reduction amongst the regional bank locations. There were plenty of ways to make an unpleasant opponent pay 'one-hundred fold', a page out of Sun Tzu's book.

On the first day of this new job, Naoto received another phone call from an old friend.

"Naoto, is this really you? Do you remember me?" came the chipper voice. "It's Kaoru Ayanokoji, from elementary school? Long time no see." Kaoru was the youngest daughter of the Ayanokoji family who ran a bathhouse next to Naoto's father's barber shop back in Nagasaki.

"Oh, Kaoru from Aya-no-yu Bathhouse? It has been a while. Where are you working now?"

"I'm actually working on the fifth floor in the Tenjin Building across the street from you!"

"Really? That's where one of our trading companies is based. You got a job at a great company."

"Your friend, Mr. Ogi, comes to our office every day for business and he invited me to a class reunion when I told him I was from Nagasaki. He mentioned your name and I hoped it was you!"

"What a small world. It must be fate. Let's have an event for all the newcomers at the bank and the trading company." So, Marunouchi Bank and Marunouchi Trading Co., Ltd., both part of the overall Marunouchi Group, held a get-together the following Friday.

Six people from the bank and four from the trading company. Amongst the attendees was a handsome new employee named Yutaka Matsuno, who would later marry Kaoru. Once the alcohol started flowing in the cozy Chinese restaurant, the ten people opened up. Naoto and Kaoru were absorbed in reminiscing about their childhood at their prestigious elementary school in the heart of Nagasaki City. Both of them had represented their school in the city-wide relay race, with Naoto taking the win on the last leg of the baton pass. The sense of victory had lingered throughout his school days.

"I remember you had moved right after that," Kaoru continued, swirling the drink in her glass. "We didn't stand a chance at the race the next year without you."

"Yeah, that was an unfortunate time." Naoto scratched at the back of his neck in embarrassment. "My father had to close his barber shop and move. I was stuck in Umegasaki all the way through high school."

Kaoru winced. "Those schools did have a reputation for delinquents. It's amazing you got into a good college. I graduated from a university in Fukuoka and spent a year at an English-language school as well."

"Perfect for applying to trading companies, especially one of the most popular amongst new graduates. I considered submitting an application too, but after the second oil crisis, the number of available positions got even lower. I'm glad I got accepted at our bank, even if it's the lowest in terms of scale and profit compared to other major banks."

"But you're working hard to improve that situation." She laughed.

"I'll keep looking at it that way," Naoto groaned and took another drink. "By the way, how are your parents doing?"

"Sadly my dad passed away from cancer around five years ago. But my mom is still doing well."

"That's a shame, my father also had a stroke and was bedridden for a while before he finally passed. My mother took care of him the whole time by herself and is still as healthy as an ox. Women of their generation are tough. Would you wanna take a drive home this weekend?" Naoto asked.

"Of course, there's a ton of pretty stops along the way, I'll put together a picnic."

While Naoto and Kaoru did catch up a lot, they also found a big difference in their values–their relationship did not deepen any further past friendship. After she got married, Kaoru quit her job and raised two children as a full-time housewife. A little while later, Naoto transferred to a branch in Kawasaki, where he remet and married Yoko, a junior high school classmate and had three children. Naoto and Kaoru went their separate ways again, not seeing each other again for nearly fifty years.

Naoto had long believed that 'love' and 'marriage' are two different things. 'Love' cannot be established without two people's strong will and positive feelings. If the love goes well, they will reach the goal of 'marriage', but if one of them feels insecure or weak-willed, it won't necessarily happen. On the other hand, marriage is truly determined by the timing and the environment (age, place, lifestyle, etc.) the two people are.

This may be the reason why marriage is said to be 'a prank of circumstance'. With romance, each person pursues their own ideals so there are very few compromises. When deciding on marriage, both parties have to be realistic and calculative.

Nearly fifty years had passed since then. Naoto started volunteering twice a week as a change of pace to avoid burnout. However, with an outbreak of coronavirus infections, he was forced to stay at home and rummage through old momentos in the attic. He found an old photo of himself and Kaoru smiling proudly after winning the relay race.

Scavenging the house for a phone book, he called up what he hoped was Kaoru's number. Indeed, her nostalgic, bright voice answered. "Hello Kaoru, it's been a while. It's Naoto."

"Naoto, really? What's wrong? Did something happen?"

"No, nothing like that. I just had some free time, so I wanted to call you. I found an old picture of us and got nostalgic, so I couldn't help it. It's been 50 years since then. How are you? Your kids?"

"I have the two of them, but it's an empty nest now."

"We had three and they're all independent now and living away from home too."

"It's good, but also lonely. My husband was in a car accident three years ago that left him brain-damaged and hospitalized, so it's lonely around here. I still go to take care of him every day though."

"That is tough," Naoto agreed. "Feel free to talk to me about anything, I've been going through the same thing. My wife developed an incurable disease eight years ago, so she's also bedridden at home. Her muscles have atrophied and her cognitive functions are almost all gone. Some days she doesn't seem to know who I am. I can't help but wonder if she's happy like this."

"Have you been taking proper care of yourself too?"

"It's fine, I'm used to it now. It's easier now that she's bedridden. When she could still walk, she would often wander off and hurt herself or hit her head. Someone would have to watch her 24/7."

"I know how that feels. You can come talk to me anytime too. We can't rush over from Kawasaki and Fukuoka, but my schedule is pretty flexible."

"Thank you, just hearing your voice again has helped so much. I'll talk to you soon."

That night, Naoto dreamt of a memory of running around a playground with a bright and lively girl.

Chapter 2 A Case of Thievery

In April 1978, Naoto was finally transferred from the 'Cost Reduction Team' he had accidentally started to the Operations and Business section. It was divided into three groups: the existing corporate transaction group, the new corporate transaction group, and the individual transaction group. Naoto was assigned to the individual transaction group and was in charge of soliciting personal deposits from medical clients, mainly private hospitals, executives of the Marunouchi corporate group, and retirees. Ogi, who had been transferred to the business department a year earlier, belonged to the existing corporate transaction group, and mainly visited large corporations with which they already had loans and other business with.

Less than half a year after Naoto was transferred, his direct superior, Section Chief Arakawa, was promoted to Chief of the Operations Section in the Saitama branch. In order to send off Arakawa, the business division had bought a fancy car and filled it with Naoto and three women from the department on the way to Fukuoka Airport. After seeing him off, the group continued to take the car for a spin, visiting clients in style.

They arrived at the mansion of an executive of

Marunouchi Trading near Ohori Park right before the company car was due back. Their business was completed quickly, but the executive's spouse kept up the small talk for much longer than expected. When they finally escaped, Naoto ran ahead to start the car. Yet, he stood there in shock–the parked car was gone. In his rush to get in and out, Naoto had left the key in the car. Maybe, someone had parked it around back for him. He couldn't find it anywhere. He tried to think it through. What if he had parked over the line, parked somewhere illegal?

He went to the nearest police station on foot, "Excuse me, I parked my car in front of Mr. Kawada's house near Ohori Park, but it's gone."

A lone police officer popped up at the front desk with an annoyed look.

"Huh? I haven't got any tow-truck reports or parking violations around here today. If it was outside somebody's house, try calling them first. We wouldn't send out a tow truck for something like this so quickly."

"If it wasn't the police, then who else could it have been?"

"Maybe you parked the car with the keys in it?" The cop asked, leaning on the desk.

"Well, yes."

"Then it was stolen, wasn't it?"

Naoto hurriedly called up the branch, "It seems like the company car has been stolen." A large number of people from the business department immediately came to the station and searched around until it got dark. In the end they could not find the car.

When he returned to the branch, Deputy Branch Manager Shimazaki was there waiting. "It's you again! What the hell are you doing? What were you thinking, parking outside with the key still in the ignition? Of course it'd get stolen! This kind of stupidity is unheard of, we just bought that car last month. You can pay us back for it. Why was a rookie like you driving around the new Lancer anyway?"

Naoto stood there silently. He had no excuse. He kneeled down on the ground and apologized to the deputy branch manager. "I'm sorry, it was my mistake. I will indeed compensate the company."

However, Shimazaki's grudge couldn't be quelled so easily.

Naoto left the dorms early in the morning to officially report the theft to the Hakata police station the next day. He arrived at the Hakata Police Station right before eight o'clock. "Sorry, my name is Naoto Yamamoto from Marunouchi Bank. I contacted you after my car was stolen near Ohori Park yesterday. I came to formally submit the incident report."

After he filled out the painfully long form, the clerk took the paper and said, "We will take the theft report today, but we'll need a representative of the company to come in again to explain. Please make an appointment."

"Wait a minute. I was the one involved, I know the situation best. I'll answer any questions, there's no need to bother anyone else."

"That's not possible. Stolen cars are often used for other crimes, so they can lead to serious incidents. So we need to ask the representative of the registered company to explain the situation."

Naoto left the Hakata police station even more disheartened, not wanting to picture Shimazaki's smug face. If the branch manager had to report to the police, the annoying deputy manager would be close behind.

As expected, Naoto's return to the office created more trouble.

"The manager doesn't have time to drive out to a little police station in the sticks to answer the same questions." Shimazaki scoffed. "I can handle it."

"It's not my rule," Naoto emphasized, feeling another headache coming on. "I'm just passing on what the officer said."

"And it has to be a joke, I'll call them up right now."

Branch manager Yamanouchi returned from a meeting just in time to hear Shimazaki shouting.

"What happened?" the manager stepped between them with his hands raised. "There's no need to yell."

Shimazaki explained in detail, ensuring that the blame remained on Naoto.

The branch manager smiled and nodded to Naoto. "It's fine, I can spare the time. Make the appointment whenever it's convenient." The difference in management style and leadership capability was clear as day between the manager and the deputy manager. The best leaders could keep their calm.

First thing the following Monday, Naoto and the branch manager arrived at the Hakata Police Station and he got to see the manager's negotiating skills firsthand. A plump, middle-aged man was the one to sit down with them. "Ah, the bankers. I'm Jiro Tomita, Chief of this department."

Naoto had to focus all his energy on not bursting out laughing at the man's ridiculous accent. It was like nothing he'd ever heard. The humor evaporated once the chief turned his attention to scolding the manager. "It's your job to properly educate your subordinates, isn't it? If you leave a car unattended with the keys in clear sight for more than an hour, it's simply asking a thief to steal it."

The manager laughed. "I can't argue that, but it's a bit of a misunderstanding. He didn't leave the car on the road, it was parked right outside our client's driveway. In that way, someone essentially trespassed on their property. Though yes, if the key hadn't been left in the car, the culprit would've had to have worked a lot harder to steal it. Yamamoto had thought that the business with said client would only take a few minutes. However, it took longer than expected, and the culprit took advantage of the opportunity."

The manager continued over the cop's attempted interruption. "It's like being involved in a car accident, Yamamoto isn't necessarily at fault. Leaving the key out in the open was responsible for motivating the theft, but it's still a crime. If your front door is unlocked, it's still unlawful for someone to barge in. We'll personally take this incident as a lesson and make sure we don't repeat such mistakes in the future."

Both Tomita and Naoto are left speechless. The manager could be ridiculously persuasive when he wanted to be–and all without yelling, unlike the deputy manager.

Tomita also nodded at the manager's words and turned to Naoto. "You lucked out this time, Mr. Yamamoto. You've been blessed with a good branch manager. I'm sure you're both busy so I won't take up any more of your time."

When they returned to the branch, the manager of the general affairs section, Azuma, called out to them. "Yamamoto, don't worry too much about it. It's just bad luck. Even so, it's a pity that you were driving the new Lancer. If it was an old one, I would have just filled out the paperwork to scrap it."

In the end, Deputy Manager Shimazaki was the only one who kept pestering Naoto for this and that. "You really tanked your hopes for career advancement with this. This theft incident is the biggest blunder since the beginning of the bank. It might be quicker to just switch jobs."

It was the direct opposite to what the Manager had said to him in the car on the way back from the station. "Don't worry too much about this. Everyone makes mistakes. Learn from them so you don't repeat them. You're young, so there's plenty of chances to make up for it. I'm sure you can do it. Good luck."

About two months later, one morning, Naoto happened to see the stolen Lancer pull up alongside him at an intersection in Tenjin. Naoto hopped off the sidewalk and rushed over to the car, politely called out to the young man who was driving. "Excuse me, but I need to talk to you. Could you pull the car over?"

The young man got out of the car leering at Naoto with suspicion.

Naoto grabbed him by the arm and questioned him in a stern tone. "Where did you get this car?"

"I bought this Lancer from a friend," the man stuttered and pulled out the vehicle inspection certificate from the glove box. However, even Naoto's untrained eye could tell it was tampered with. Naoto grabbed him by the arm and forcibly took him all the way to the Hakata Police Station. After an investigation, it was determined that this was indeed Naoto's stolen car, and that the culprits were him and his friend.

Chief Tomita at that time said to Naoto, "You've done a good job. Now your failures have been erased. I hope you can live up to that manager of yours' expectations."

Chapter 3 Forward Exchange Contracts

After working in the business department at the Fukuoka branch, Naoto moved on to the loan department for about a year and five months, and then on May 25, 1979, he received another transfer order. That same day, Naoto's boss, Loan Manager Sekimoto, sent Naoto off to Branch Manager Yamanouchi's office as soon as he entered the office. He found Yamanouchi and deputy manager Shimazaki hunched over a table in conversation.

"Yamamoto, you've been transferred. Congratulations. Your next branch is in Motosumiyoshi," the manager said cheerfully, Shimazaki scowling behind him.

Naoto was a country boy and had no idea where Motosumiyoshi was. It reminded him of Osaka for some reason.

"Thank you very much…Is that in the Osaka area?" Naoto asked hesitantly.

"Osaka?" Shimazaki laughed. "It's a branch in Kanagawa. You know Kanagawa, Yokohama? Tokyo? A completely different region? You need to study more about our bank, it's one of the biggest private branches!"

The branch manager explained in detail. "The Motosumiyoshi branch is a very profitable office that was recently featured in the weekly magazine 'Shincho' as the branch with the highest growth in personal deposits among banks in the country. It might be the perfect branch for you. Keep up the good work."

"Sorry, I've lived in the sticks in Nagasaki my whole life, so I only really know where the ones in Kyushu are. I apologize that I need to catch up." Naoto followed up with a slew of detailed questions that shut Shimazaki up for the moment–at least that man didn't know the answers either.

Naoto was a little disappointed when he heard that it was only a medium-sized store that mainly dealt with individual customers. His goal when entering the company was to deal with corporate partners, large accounts with other businesses. Thankfully, the first Fukuoka branch he worked in had been a corporate store, just as Naoto had hoped. One day he'd do work that would lead to the development of venture companies that were expected to grow in the future and lead to their listing on the stock exchange. However, when he actually arrived at the Motosumiyoshi branch, he found that it was not a typical private store.

More than 90% of the approximately 200 business partners who took over from his predecessor were corporations. Among them, there were more than 30 venture companies with state-of-the-art technology to produce semiconductors. All had a ton of potential that he was more than willing to feed.

It was going to be interesting. The Motosumiyoshi branch initially started as a branch centered around individual transactions, but as the Japanese economy entered a period of rapid growth, technological companies in the area expanded their business. And Naoto was transferred right at the apex of this innovation. It was an era of regulated interest rate deposits right before the approaching liberalization of interest rates, and the performance of a branch was still evaluated according to how much individual deposits it collected. The Motosumiyoshi branch's performance in regards to personal deposits was unmatched by other branches. It had received the highly-coveted 'president's award' for eight consecutive terms. It was a branch with the momentum to drop a soaring bird.

Unlike the large Fukuoka branch, the atmosphere inside Motosumiyoshi was familial and lively, with only a total of about 50 employees. Naoto had about a year and a half of experience in foreign exchange loans under his belt, so he was assigned to the same foreign exchange loan section at the new branch, taking over the duties from his predecessor. Naoto was the youngest among the managers and deputy managers with four seniors above him. Hiroshi Arai, who was one year older, Osamu Nakayama, two years senior, then Masato Tomikawa and Tadashi Shibayama were both three years older.

At that time, the Japanese economy was supported by a huge boom and was experiencing rapid growth against the backdrop of a strong yen and high stock prices, so the corporate demand for funds was strong. The Bank of Japan had already begun restricting the total amount allowed in order to curb excessive bank lending. At the sales floor, workers struggled to somehow meet the demand for funds from their corporate clients, while balancing the strict lending limits imposed by the head office and government. This unfortunately continued and Naoto and the others were unable to fully respond to their clients' requests. From the beginning of the term, the lending section of each branch had repeated hard negotiations with the head office's credit department over the loan limit. Even so, it still wasn't possible to meet the demands. Instead, they shifted from 'yen' loans that had already been lent to customers to 'foreign currency' loans'. These new loans were not subject to the Bank of Japan's lending limit regulations.

For example, to briefly explain the scheme of this new plan, the 10 billion yen loan that had been lent to a certain business partner was replaced with an equivalent amount of a foreign currency, like dollars. By doing this, the yen lending frame would be worked out for three months. However, since the exchange rate would fluctuate during a span of three months, there was a risk of suffering an unexpected exchange loss. At that time, the exchange rate was accelerating and the yen was stronger than ever.

Therefore, going forward, exchange contracts were more advantageous to customers the later they were. The three-month-futures contract exchange rate was 170 yen to the dollar—in other words, in order to raise 56 million dollars, you would need about 9.5 billion yen, which is the difference between 10 billion yen and 500 million yen. In theory it was a good deal, but the profit and loss statements would be chaotic due to the interest rate difference between Japan and the US. However, if the exchange rate fluctuated in the opposite direction, such as a depreciation of the yen against the dollar, unexpected losses could occur. Therefore, it was essential to enter into a forward buying contract in advance in order to mitigate such loss risk.

At the time, everyone expected the yen to appreciate against the dollar, not a single foreign exchange analyst would have denied this prediction. The people in charge of the lending and foreign exchange departments of each branch claimed that the longer the forward exchange contract is delayed, the more the yen would appreciate—therefore, the more exchange profit would be generated by the corporate client. So nearly all clients and their bank correspondents procrastinated enacting the loans as long as possible. However, in 1982, this excessive 'strong yen against the dollar' suddenly reversed.

Tomikawa, Naoto's senior coworker, hastily reported to Manager Ikeya, one of the most reliable people in the building.

"Mr. Ikeya, three months ago, we asked Kanagawa LP Gas to change their existing yen loan to a foreign currency loan. With the appreciation of the yen against the dollar at that time, we had put off the foreign exchange contract for the dollar fund when we repaid the loan. But now, the sudden depreciation of the yen has screwed us over. If we continue at this rate, we will lose about 56 million yen to our business partners. We ended up incurring the foreign exchange loss, despite what we predicted. I'm sorry."

Ikeya was surprised by his report. "What? Why didn't you make a forward exchange contract right away? Who the hell made that decision?" He gathered everyone together and checked to see if there were any other transactions that had not been forwarded right away. It turned out that only Naoto and Nakayama hadn't procrastinated forwarding their many exchange contracts. Of course, Ikeya was fully aware that the ultimate responsibility for this rested with him, the management. He'd been having trouble sleeping and feeling irritable lately, and this only exacerbated these health problems. There were two possible countermeasures against this unexpected loss. One was to implement the forward exchange contracts immediately to fix the exchange loss from then on. Yet, in this case, the bank would bear the full loss of 56 million yen. In that case, the person in charge would bear the primary responsibility, the manager of the foreign exchange section would bear the administrative responsibility, and the branch manager would bear the left over amount. Considering this, Mr. Ikeya couldn't imagine that the three of them could handle that loss.

Mr. Ikeya drummed his fingers on his desktop, locked away in his office, murmuring out loud. "The person in charge, Tomikawa, will need to be fired. But he still has two young children. If we sit still and wait for the yen to potentially appreciate and cover it all up without reporting it to the branch manager, there's a high possibility that I'll be dismissed as an accomplice in the same way as Tomikawa...We'd both be thrown under the bus." Ikeya held his head in his palms.

In the end, Ikeya went to work first thing in the morning and reported everything that had happened up to that point to the branch manager. Neither of them came out of the office for hours. The Loan and Foreign Exchange Division went from its normal harmonious atmosphere to a morose and silent office. After 5 o'clock, both men were summoned to the head office and didn't return to Motosumiyoshi until midnight. All employees related to these accounts could not go home until their meetings were over. Naoto was lucky enough to walk home, since the company housing was only one station over, but the others had to take a taxi home since it was past the last train. And of course, said taxi fare was paid by the individual, not the office. This lifestyle somehow continued on for about two months, and Arai, Tomikawa, and Shibayama finally began to think about changing jobs. They used their days off to take exams for mid-career hires at securities companies and insurance companies to prepare for the worst. Two months later, the Human Resources Department finally came to a conclusion.

"The branch manager and the loan and foreign exchange manager will be admonished, and the three members of the section will be severely reprimanded." This was the final disciplinary action issued by the Human Resources Department. However, considering the actual loss of 56,000,000 yen, there was no way that such a slap on the wrist would be enough.

In fact, a few days after the announcement, Naoto was taken aside by the branch manager. "The personnel department has something to ask you, so I'd like you to go to the personnel department with me to talk it over."

Three days later, after they finally finished their regular work at 8:00 p.m., Naoto and the branch manager went to the interview with the personnel department. The branch manager stepped out during the actual interview, discussing something with the personnel manager. The two staff members left behind began asking Naoto question after question. Another person in the room scribbled down every word Naoto said.

"We will decide on the punishment for the people involved in this scandal," one of them started, "but before that, I would like to ask for your opinion on a few matters. Who was in good standing with the exchange contracts? What was the situation at that time? Did each person decide to withhold the foreign exchange contracts on their own, or did one of the three take the lead? Also, why did this scandal occur? Even if it's just your personal opinion, I'd like you to tell us what you think about the cause."

Taken aback by the barrage of questions, Naoto made note that he had to choose his words carefully–he didn't want to accidentally sell out his coworkers. "As for the first question, I work with the three of them, but I don't have a chance to see their work every day. As for your second point, why did this scandal occur? It's a matter of debate, but why did our branches ask their close business partners to change their existing yen loans to foreign currency loans? So they could find a loophole in complying with the Bank of Japan's regulations for capping the lending amount allowed. In response to the Bank of Japan's mandates, the screening department from headquarters narrowed down the lending limit for each branch. But for those of us on the sales floor, we still had to somehow meet the financial needs of our customers. We were the ones to ask our close business partners to change their existing yen loans to foreign currency loans, trying to act in their best interests while also obeying the rules. I think that I should have grasped the actual situation properly and helped out more. More specifically, if headquarters had consolidated the forward exchange contracts of all associated branches on the day following their execution, I believe that this scandal wouldn't have occurred." Naoto bit his tongue at the staff's expressions, but had to continue on with his frank opinion. "By doing so, I think we would have been able to reduce the clerical burden as well as not having each branch office make their own judgments about future exchange rates. There's also the issue of foreign exchange administrative procedures. These trades are clearly different from normal trades, and should be treated as so. What's different is that this transaction is mostly for the bank's convenience. So it would make sense if the administrative procedures could be less laborious. In other words, in order to reduce the clerical burden of those in charge of the branch, it should have been necessary to take measures, such as reviewing the system so transactions could be carried out automatically. The third measure would be to have the fund exchange department check the foreign exchange transactions at branches more frequently. The Treasury Department is supposed to manage the daily positions of future exchanges for the entire bank, including these branch offices. Finally, I have a request for the Human Resources Department. I doubt this problem is unique to the Motosumiyoshi branch. A fact-finding survey for all branches should be conducted as soon as possible. And if this problem is common to most branches, then as I said earlier, rather than treating it as a misconduct by an individual, I think the inaction of the headquarters should be held responsible."

The room was silent, with only the rapid scratch of the notetaker's pen. The man asking the questions leaned over to his partner and barely audibly said, "Let's get the fact-finding survey together right away and assign people to each branch! Send a letter of inquiry addressed to all branch managers under the name of the personnel manager."

They thanked Naoto in unison for his time and help. Weeks later, Naoto was able to read the results of the survey— it was found that most branches had similar transactions and issues.

As a result, lighter-than-usual punishments for the six people from the Motosumiyoshi branch were accepted with a blind eye. When this problem came to light, Naoto knew from the beginning that the problem was not just his branch office, but in the headquarters and their inaction.

The branch manager came up to him with a curious look the day after the impromptu interview. "Yamamoto, what did you say to the personnel manager the other night? He called me and said that he wanted to transfer you to their planning department…"

Two months later, on April 1, 1987, Naoto received the official notice to transfer to the planning department in the bank's headquarters.

Chapter 4 Tsukishima Branch

Naoto was transferred from the Motosumiyoshi branch to the planning department at Marunouchi Bank's headquarters. Specifically, he was assigned as a liaison to the Ministry of Finance. During his time in this position, he would confront the authorities about the faulty 'convoy system', be involved in the bank's listing on the New York Stock Exchange, and assist with the management integration with Tokyo Nihonbashi Bank. One day, after several years and all of the said accomplishments, Naoto was called into the head office.

"Yamamoto, you've been transferred. Congratulations on becoming the deputy manager of the Tsukishima branch. For your future advancement, I thought it would be best for you to take a closer look at the actual situation of our current sales site. However, it will be for about two years."

"Eh? Why that long?"

"Isn't it obvious? I don't know what we'll do with you at this branch any longer, and it would be terrible if the new employees here were influenced by you, the manager joked. "Besides, it looks like the bubble economy is about to burst. If we time it right, you'll be back here in the planning department exactly as the banking industry might be in big trouble."

"Understood," Naoto relinquished. "Then I'll do my best for those two years."

In this way, Naoto was appointed as the deputy branch manager of the Tsukishima Branch, which was located near the Tokyo Metro Yurakucho Line, not a far move. The branch had a total of 14 employees since it was a new branch that only opened two years ago, mainly for individual transactions. The branch manager was Koji Yamashita, who joined the bank in 1969. Under him was Naoto as the deputy branch manager, the sales section manager Tadashi Hasebe, the operation section manager Toshiharu Yamada, the loan section manager Tsuneo Oda, and the deputy section manager Kazumi Oike. There were four other men and four other women working under them.

The day Naoto was scheduled to arrive, the tiny office buzzed with everyone's guesses at what kind of corporate stuffed-shirt would be sent from the head office. Naoto himself walked up to the building equally as nervous. He had hopes for a warm welcome, but that naive notion was blown away once he stepped through the door.

Naoto had little experience working at a branch focused on individual customers, after spending most of his career going through company clients, and as the deputy branch manager he was the second in every decision. He was more or less left on his own to figure things out. It was daunting, but he honestly preferred it, not being stuck in someone else's rut.

In one of his first weeks, a man with an extraordinarily strong physique came into their office.

"Hello, what can we do for you today?" Junko Kawamura, a newbie working as a teller, called out to the man and waved him over.

Without any preface, he whipped out a check and his savings account passbook. "Please deposit this check for 10 billion yen into my account."

"Yes, right away," Junko stuttered, fumbling for the check far larger than what she was used to dealing with. The payment process went through immediately. "Thank you very much. By the way, did you know our bank is offering a new product, 'My Card Loan'? It makes it much more convenient to withdraw cash up to 200,000 yen in an emergency. This application only requires your name and date of birth on the form, and we can have it available right away."

While listening to this interaction, Naoto was concerned that Junko had forgotten part of the usual sales pitch–when applying for this product, there was a screening process, and we may not be able to accept it. This was because card loans were credit (lending) transactions, and not a product that just anyone can use. In theory, Naoto had long wondered whether it was okay to sell such products to an unspecified number of people at a deposit counter. It could get out of hand really easily.

The man filled out the application form on the spot and handed it back to her.

"Thank you very much. We'll send you a loan card through registered mail. It'll take about two weeks to issue the card, so please wait until then."

When the man was about to leave, he turned and asked, "Can I withdraw the 10,000,000 yen check I just deposited tomorrow?"

"You can withdraw the amount in the afternoon two business days from the date of deposit."

However, first thing in the morning the following Monday, the same man called the branch in a huff. "Is there a branch manager? I demand to talk to the branch manager!"

The veteran sales manager Hasebe answered the phone. "I'm sorry. The branch manager has a meeting at the head office this morning and is out for the day. My name is Mr. Hasebe, the sales manager, I can take care of it for you."

"I guess that'll work," the man sighed. "Actually, I deposited a check for 10 million yen with a teller last Friday, and I asked the lady 'When can I withdraw this?' and she said I could take it out the next day. So that's why I tried to buy gold on Sunday, but no matter how many times I tried to use my card, the cash wouldn't come out. In the end, I couldn't buy any, and the price of gold skyrocketed today. If I had bought it on Sunday, I would have made over a million yen. So I'm holding you responsible for that loss. I'm coming over there right now!"

Hasebe consulted with Naoto in a panic.

Naoto thought for a few moments. "Manager, when would you normally cash a check that was deposited last Friday?"

"A 10,000,000 yen check brought in on Friday would be exchanged and settled on Monday, the next business day. So if it was honored, they would be able to withdraw cash on Monday afternoon. However, if the bank from which the check was drawn does not have the cash ready, it would be 'dishonored' and canceled as if no deposit had been made on Friday in the first place."

He sighed. "Okay. Then, what time today will we find out if the 10 million yen check has been dishonored?"

"It'll be back from the clearing house at two o'clock at the latest."

Naoto gradually came to understand the trap that man had set. In other words, the man brought in a check for 10 million yen, which was taken without any cash in the first place, to our bank last Friday, and he was fully aware of it. The dishonor would be revealed this afternoon, so he might have tried to blackmail us out of the money by claiming that he had lost money in the transaction.

Junko at the counter had been used as an excuse for the complaint. When he asked her, 'When can I withdraw this check?', he selfishly interpreted 'two *business* days later' as 'two days later'.

"Let's buy some time until 2 o'clock," Naoto instructed, "then we can confirm his scam." Naoto's strategy worked brilliantly, and they were able to distract him until the dishonor was officially sent. With the hard evidence, the man gave up on the blackmail and ran out before the police could arrive. Naoto and Hasebe assumed that meant the matter was settled, but two weeks later the same man filed another complaint.

"Are you guys making fun of me? What the hell is this postcard?" The man rushed into the bank like a hurricane. Hasebe jumped up to usher him to the reception room when other customers started looking worried.

"I don't even wanna talk about it. The other day, the lady at the window told me to apply for your loan card, so I filled out the application."

The following was written on the postcard. 'Thank you for choosing us for your financial needs. Unfortunately, we're writing to inform you that we will not be able to accept your application after further examination.'

"I only signed those papers because she forced me to! What's with this condescending rejection? Tell me why exactly I didn't pass."

Hasebe jumped slightly at the man's threatening body language. "I'm...I'm not sure I have the authority to look into that. Please wait while I get the deputy manager."

Once again Naoto had to drop his other work to confront this man–though this time he had an actual point. As Naoto listened to his complaints, he thought about the best way to word, 'you were rejected because you're a known-extortionist and involved in organized crime.'

"Sir, I did overhear your discussion with our employee about the My Card Loan product at the time, so I admit the pitch was not well-explained. This product has to be reviewed by higher-ups at the bank, so it may not be accepted. I understand your anger, there is no excuse for the miscommunication on our part."

The man finally relaxed in his seat. "That's right. You could've apologized honestly like that from the beginning. Unlike the sales manager, you understand what you're talking about. It's dangerous to carry around large amounts of cash when buying gold, so I'm thinking of using a check. Could you open a checking account for me?"

This must have been his original intention–what might convince him to give up on the offer.

"I understand. Then could you prepare these documents for consideration right away so we can submit the paperwork."

"Oh, yes. You're much more sensible, I'll have to deal with you directly next time. What papers do you need?"

From here on, it was Naoto's playing field. "First of all,

can I have your tax returns with the stamp of the tax office from the past three years? We'll check the purchase and earnings status, and that there are no unpaid or delinquent taxes, such as resident or property taxes. So please go to the government office and get a 'tax payment certificate'. Then, please submit your resume and work history. Also, please include information about your immediate family. Since the drawing of a check or bill is equivalent to a bank lending money, we will have to take our time reviewing it."

The man scribbled down the list of necessary documents, but eventually he got frustrated and stood up in a flurry. "This is ridiculous, I'll be back another time."

Yet after that, he never returned. Japan's 'lost decade' when the bubble economy finally burst began in earnest at that time in 1992. Naoto had been appointed to the Tsukishima branch in May 1991 when all the banks were still trying to increase their lending.

The headquarters of Marunouchi Bank had previously developed new products, such as Good Balloons, which were super long-term (15 to 20 years) loans that did not have to be repaid every month. Headquarters put quotas for the sales team to push them. Naoto had had a heated discussion with the person in charge of the business planning department while they were developing the product. "This kind of high-risk financial product may sell well during a bubble like the one we have now, but when the economy deteriorates and the business conditions for our customers deteriorate, it can cause fatal problems."

And he had been right. The reality of a mountain of bad debts buried them.

When a new branch, like the Tsukishima one, opens, approval from the Ministry of Finance is necessary and an 'opening preparation committee' is hired. From these people, a branch manager will be picked based on their performance and experience. Back at headquarters, the department in charge of branch operations formulates a plan for the grand opening. As a result of these efforts, the Tsukishima branch performed well in its first year and was selected for an award.

However, one year after the opening of the store the transfer of excellent personnel from the first generation began. The loan manager was the first to be replaced, followed by the deputy branch manager. With all of the accolades, these managers all went on to bigger promotions, leaving the Tsukishima branch with only new people fumbling around. Trying to regain a hold on the reins, Naoto scoffed at these pointless performance evaluations. In other words, he had big doubts about the outdated and ambiguous evaluation criteria used to hand out awards.

At the third anniversary of the branch's opening, Naoto caught sight of one of the evaluators at the party–the perfect time to voice these complaints. "Thank you very much for taking time out of your busy schedules to attend today's celebration of the third anniversary of the opening of the Tsukishima branch," Naoto began. I would like to express my heartfelt gratitude to all of you for attending. I would like to make a proposal from the branch office, and that is regarding the criterion for the 'increase in loan volume'. This was the most important criterion in the performance evaluation of new branches in the branch department this past year. Under the perception that lending volume is directly linked to 'profit.' So I have one question. The Tsukishima branch's increase in loans this fiscal year was 30th out of the 36 new branches, which is a disappointing result. However, our 'net profit' is not included in the evaluation criteria. In terms of this important index, we have achieved unrivaled results. Why is the Tsukishima branch not an award-winning store?"

The branch manager jumped to answer the hypothetical Naoto posed, worried that the executives present at the celebration would affect their evaluation. He began to speak confidently, "Simple, the branch performance evaluation standard adopted by headquarters is not based on 'net profit' but rather 'business profit', which is said to best represent the results of the efforts from that period. If you evaluate with net profit, it would include the loan write-offs that occur when a business partner goes bankrupt. Isn't it cruel to make the branch manager at that time bear the full responsibility for that?"

Naoto thought, the small crowd around them muttering. "I see, you have a point there." But he couldn't let it die there. "Let's look at it from a slightly different perspective. Currently, the asset bubble is at its peak, but isn't it only a matter of time before it bursts? Once the bubble bursts, it's likely that loan write-offs will occur from corporate bankruptcies and other factors. In that case, let's say that a branch is evaluated for its business profit, which doesn't include these loan write-offs, and becomes an award-winning branch. On the other hand, unlike the Tsukishima branch, although the operating profit is not so large, there's almost no loan write-off, so the net profit is the same amount. Under the current standards of the branch department, one branch is evaluated as an award-winning branch, and the other is evaluated as unsuccessful. Is this evaluation really an accurate representation of the financial status of the branch?"

The branch manager held his head. The executive listening in asked Naoto a question instead. "I see, in a sense what you are saying makes sense. We can't just let the branch manager take the blame."

"And which profit pays your executive compensation? Is it from the current profit, including all expenses?" The officer remained silent, Naoto continued to insist. "Executives know this, don't they? You're also bank employees, so they should be well aware of these basics. Then, when loan write-offs skyrocket, do you executives receive executive compensation just because you are earning 'business profits' despite having no financial resources? There is a risk that this is a breach of trust under the Commercial Code. It is time to correct these evaluation standards."

Everyone around them fell into an awkward silence, and the atmosphere of the celebration suddenly subsided. However, Naoto could not continue to let things go unnoticed. He had to give back to the bank that had nurtured him through his career thus far. The Tsukishima branch of Marunouchi Bank was a small new branch, and the Tsukishima branch of Mitsuwa Bank was already established in the same area. The Mitsuwa Bank branch was a large-scale store compared to the Marunouchi one. As soon as Naoto transferred to the Tsukishima branch, he set up an appointment with the branch manager of Mitsuwa Bank Tsukishima branch. He had heard that the branch was more than five times the size of his and that it probably had over 100 employees.

At the appointment, Naoto was told to wait for the manager to finish up with the previous client. It ended up being more than 30 minutes before the secretary led him up to the office, introducing Naoto as if he had only just arrived. The older man stood up to greet him, and he couldn't shake the feeling that he had met him somewhere. The two exchanged business cards–Mitsuwa Bank, Managing Director Tsukishima Branch Manager, Kou Tanabe. Later, Naoto found out Tanabe was eventually promoted up the ranks to the president of Mitsuwa Bank. During his future tenure as president, he was an amazing manager who pushed Mitsuwa Bank to the top position amongst city banks in terms of all of the 'operating income', 'ordinary income', and 'net income', which were said to be the triple crown of profits. That would be more than fifteen years before executives were arrested for avoiding financial inspections.

Around this time, Mitsuwa Bank was known as both the 'People's Bank' and elites in the banking industry–both Mitsuwa and Marunouchi were fighting for the top position against Igeta Bank, another in the Kansai area. Naoto was confident that Marunouchi would eventually pull ahead because of its corporate culture and employee education. At that time, the bank supervisory authorities were still managing by means of a 'convoy system', so there was not much difference between the lending limit and the number of branches.

Tanabe tapped his pen and stared Naoto down as well. Eventually, he exclaimed, "That's right! When Marunouchi Bank was going to list on the New York Stock Exchange and came to the Ministry of Finance for a hearing. I remember you giving a long speech on behalf of your planning department."

"It was such a big competition for all the major commercial

banks to see who could be the first to list on the New York Stock Exchange. Mitsuwa Bank was one of the earliest to set up a project team to go public. The officer at that time called us naive and said we'd regret it later." Naoto shook his head. "And yet, the same man gave us the roundabout advice that if our financial statements were to be prepared according to US GAAP, the company would be in the red and couldn't be listed. It was rough, but in the end it really helped us break up the convoy system and establish ourselves amongst giants like your bank. And I remember it was you that said 'I hope you don't regret your choice'."

Tanabe nodded along. "You were indeed spunky then. I'm surprised to now see you demoted to this tiny branch. Did you offend someone?"

Naoto coughed out a laugh. Just a few days after he was transferred, Marunouchi President Wakata called him to his office along with Vice President Kishimoto to congratulate him on the 'promotion'. Wakata was cracking up, but Kishimoto had a sour expression.

"While this transfer might not be a promotion," Kishimoto had explained, "but it's not a punishment or a retraining. What you brought up at the board meeting, about slowing down on the loans the bank was handing out. We need management like you to help change our lending policy across the branches. You can help us prepare for the inevitable economic collapse.

Figure out how to revitalize our business partners."

"I wasn't demoted as much as sent to inspect and teach the smaller branches. Kind of rehabilitate them," Naoto said, shaking off the Vice President's old instructions. "Mr. Tanabe, you know what will happen from here on, don't you? The foreign exchange options sold at your branch have increased your losses due to the recent depreciation of the yen, and your clients are about to go bankrupt. Not only that, but the entire banking industry is bound to face a management crisis. Our most urgent issue is to rebuild our client companies that have already started to decline as soon as possible."

Tanabe's teasing expression grew serious. He closed his eyes for a moment and said, "It's already too late. If we'd realized this a year earlier and taken action, we might have managed somehow, but there's nothing we can do about it now. We can't turn back." Tanabe had already foreseen what would happen to the banking industry as a manager, but had done too little too late.

"That's not completely true. From now on you should return to your headquarters and see how far you can steer the ship away from the crisis. I'm going to do my best to do damage control too. I don't know what the next ten years will hold, but please take care of yourself."

Soon after that conversation, the 'lost decade' began. Mitsuwa bowed to Toyo Bank and merged into UBJ Bank.

Later, in 2006, Marunouchi Bank would absorb UBJ and form Tokyo Marunouchi Bank. Unbeknownst to everyone at the Tsukishima branch, Naoto worked behind the scenes to curb the excessive lending promotion policy of the bubble era, leaving them with less debt than other branches. Fortunately, the main branch manager, Mr. Yamashita, was the type to leave most of the tedious work to the deputy manager, so Naoto was able to carry out this work as he wished.

Yamashita was an elite graduate from Kyoto University who joined the bank in 1969. He had a lot of experience in overseas branches and was good at dealing with large companies. However, he was not very familiar with dealing with Japanese small and medium-sized companies, and that weakness was reflected in his management style. Naoto had first met him on a business trip to the Brussels branch in Belgium. The local Japanese employees held a welcome party for Naoto, and it lasted late into the night.

When Naoto was about to turn in for the night, Yamashita rushed over and whispered, "Yamamoto, can you play mahjong? Let's play a round."

Naoto had to turn him down since his sleep was already disrupted from jet lag, leaving him off on the wrong foot with Yamashita. The man was so fond of mahjong that he later took the initiative to make a club with the corporate clients at the Tsukishima branch.

When Yamashita moved on, the next manager was Hidekazu Matsubara, who joined the bank in 1971 and graduated from Keio University. Like Yamashita, he didn't have much experience dealing with domestic, smaller companies, leaving Naoto stuck in the man's office explaining various concepts for hours.

At one point, Naoto inevitably got into an argument with him.

"I have a meeting with corporate next week," Matsubara started, "but there is no problem if I say we'll be able to achieve the target of increasing loans of 1 billion yen for this term, right?"

"I don't think it's possible," Naoto repeated. "We haven't even reached half of our goal. It's nearly impossible to increase loans by over 500 million yen in the next two months. We should focus on rebuilding our business partners instead. The bubble is about to burst. If we don't start rebuilding our business partners soon, it will be a big problem later. By the way, how was this target of 1 billion yen set? It's a figure calculated by adding 20 percent of the average growth rate of a new store group to the results of its previous term. But it doesn't take into consideration the trends of the Japanese economy or the special circumstances that differ at each branch. Is it really fair? I was in charge of company briefings for investors in the planning department, but I never disclosed figures like that. The most important information for an investor is the profit target, after deducting loan write-offs, etc. Since it's directly linked to the capital adequacy ratio, which determines the evaluation of the bank. This would be a better standard, and I don't care as much about hitting these arbitrary targets."

Matsubara remained silent. Naoto couldn't reveal his 'secret mission', so he went about it in a roundabout way. "It could be easy to meet the loan target. If we change directions and look for new corporate clients, we can easily achieve one or two billion in new loans. However, if we do that when the bubble is about to burst, the next generation will bear a huge loss. Therefore, rather than increasing new lending, I think it's necessary to work on rebuilding existing business partners. Let them compete in performance evaluations to see how they can avoid delaying losses onto the next generation."

"I see," Matsubara conceded after a breath, "your argument is justified. However, as long as we work within an organization, we have no choice but to follow the rules. So that hypothetical is moot."

"But if someone doesn't take responsibility now, nothing will change no matter how long we delay. Any branch manager, no matter how unreasonable the goals of the headquarters, will want to improve their short-term performance and raise their evaluation during their term of office."

When Matsubara returned from the meeting at headquarters

the next week, he was high on righteous confrontation. "Mr. Yamamoto, I told the team your thoughts. They threatened to demote me when I insisted, but I said to him, 'No matter where you demote me, we'll all be in trouble unless someone speaks up'."

Naoto looked at him, too surprised for words. Maybe he could become a manager who could be entrusted with steering the ship. He was ready to share a concrete plan, starting by classifying existing customers into three categories, A, B, or C, according to their current business conditions. A would be an excellent company with no problems in their business conditions, B would be a company that needs attention due to deteriorating business conditions, and C would be a company with a high risk of bankruptcy. Of course, as for the new business, we focused on companies classified as A and worked carefully from there. In the morning, Naoto, together with the person in charge of new corporate clients, conducted outreach activities focusing on these A clients, and in the afternoon, visited the business partners classified as B and C, proposing various restructuring measures to them–such as increasing sales by introducing business partners, reducing borrowings by selling idle real estate, integrating management, and reviewing executive compensation.

In the two years since he was appointed to the Tsukishima branch, Naoto supported the restructuring of about 100 business partners classified as B or C, and none of them fell into bankruptcy. Matsubara finally understood Naoto's ideas, and was no longer obsessed with the performance evaluation targets for the branch office. He finally understood Naoto's mission to prepare for the long-term losses that would occur when the bubble burst.

However, as pointed out by the Mitsuwa Bank branch manager Tanabe, it was an undeniable fact that such measures were too late. They were not even halfway out from under the rubble. After Naoto's promised two years, Matsubara handed over his transfer. "Thank you for your hard work over the past two years. I'm sure you feel like you still have a lot to do. I hope you take this valuable experience and use it for the benefit of the entire bank."

Chapter 5 Financial Crisis

In 1992, the Japanese economy fell from prosperity and stock and real estate prices began to plummet. In the securities industry, Yamaichi Securities went bankrupt. In the banking industry, the government-affiliated Nippon Credit Bank and Long-Term Bank of Japan went bankrupt. Among city banks, Hokkaido Takushoku Bank went bankrupt, and local banks, such as Ashikaga Bank, dominoed one after another. In order to stop the rapid increase in bad loans, the Ministry of Finance decided to write off bad loans at once, and instructed the Kanto Bankers Association to consider urgent measures. In order to dispose of a huge amount of non-performing loans at once, a large amount of funds for write-offs was required. Kishimoto, the newly-appointed president of the Tokyo Marunouchi Bank, asked Naoto if there was a way to raise funds for this depreciation. As chairman of the Kanto Bankers Association, he appealed to banks nationwide that if they did not 'dispose' of their bad loans as soon as possible, they would be in big trouble.

"Yamamoto, at the request of a major politician from the Liberal People's Party, the Ministry of Finance assessed various land owned by companies at market value in order to deal with the rapidly increasing bad debts in one go. It seems like they're trying to use the surplus profit that doesn't appear on the accounting books as a source of write-offs."

"It'd be effective temporarily, but real estate prices are currently declining as well. If it continues at this rate, unrealized losses (losses that do not appear in the accounting books where the market value is lower than the book value) will be everywhere. It would be a double-edged sword."

"Indeed, this might come back to haunt us later. I'm at a loss. Do you have any other ideas?"

Naoto had been contemplating ways to raise the funds to dispose of bad debts for a while, but had kept it close to the chest. However, the best method he had come up with had an extremely high hurdle–the ultra-conservative wall of the Ministry of Justice. "There is one way, but not a lot of people will go for it. We need to introduce 'tax effect accounting'. Of course, this would apply not only to the banking industry, but to all Japanese companies, so the only big negotiation would be with the Ministry of Finance. We'd need to convince the Ministry of Justice to accept it too. Then we'll be able to generate several tens of trillions of yen worth of funds for depreciation."

In addition to administrative guidance for the banking and insurance industries, the Ministry of Finance also had jurisdiction over the securities industry, with the Securities and

Exchange Audit Commission under its umbrella. However, their scope is limited to companies listed on the stock exchange, mainly large companies that only account for 0.3 percent of companies. On the other hand, the Ministry of Justice had jurisdiction over the Commercial Code, which applied to all 3,674,000 Japanese companies, thus the majority of Japanese companies.

Naoto had dealt with the Ministry of Justice once before regarding the merger of the Marunouchi Bank and the Tokyo Nihonbashi Bank. It was a consultation about the value of the business when the surviving bank, Marunouchi Bank, absorbed the assets of Tokyo Nihonbashi Bank. At that time, Naoto had had a lot of trouble persuading Hideo Murata, a formidable assistant manager, about introducing 'tax effect accounting'. However, the current financial crisis was not a situation in which such leniency could be tolerated.

"Ah, the banker who was so mouthy back at the Ministry. I remember it well." Murata raised an eyebrow at him. "So what's your business today? I don't have much time."

"Let me just take a few minutes of your time. "As you know, the banking industry is currently receiving demands from the government to expedite the disposal of non-performing loans. In order to generate some cash, we're asking if the 'tax effect accounting', which is already permitted in the Securities and Exchange Act settlement, could also be accepted in the

Commercial Law settlement.

"Mr. Yamamoto, you know very well why the Ministry of Justice hasn't accepted that yet. Unlike the Securities and Exchange Law, the Ministry of Justice cannot accept the application of such sloppy tax effect accounting to the settlement of accounts under the Commercial Code. It's a whole other ballpark."

Naoto had expected this kind of pushback. After the rejection, he had to take the train ride home to restrategize.

The point of this accounting method was to recognize in advance the expected tax saving effect, and then record that amount on the balance sheet as 'deferred tax assets'. Therefore, the counterpart on the balance sheet for deferred tax assets capitalized is 'profit', which then becomes the source of amortization for disposal of bad debts. It was already allowed to be voluntarily applied in the Securities and Exchange Act, which was mandatory for large companies. Yet for the majority of small and medium-sized companies, it was only required to prepare financial statements based on the Commercial Code. In other words, there was no way to convince the Ministry of Justice without roping in all of those majority of small and medium-sized enterprises. It was time to take this story to the National Federation of Economic Organizations and gain public recognition. With the bursting of the bubble economy, most Japanese companies were suffering from deficits. So, if that could somehow be manipulated to be recorded as profit, it would help not only the banking industry, but the entire drowning economy.

Naoto took the plunge and raised this issue at the Finance Committee of the National Federation of Economic Organizations, where he was a regular attendee. As expected, the companies who were members jumped at the proposal. Soon enough, the Ministry of International Trade and Industry (now the Ministry of Economy, Trade, and Industry) teamed up with the Ministry of Finance to overwhelm the Ministry of Justice.

In October 1998, tax effect accounting was finally introduced into the settlement of accounts under the Commercial Code. At that time, 'deferred tax assets' recorded on the balance sheets of financial institutions amounted to more than 10 trillion yen. The same amount of profit was generated and became the source of funds for the disposal of bad loans, lifting a weight off the economy all at once. With this, many Japanese banks thought they'd be able to avoid a financial crisis, but there were unexpected side effects related to their operation. With the change in policy, the accounting audit industry was now involved, and the Minister for Financial Affairs Takeda was cracking down. As a result, banks that were accused of 'overstating' deferred tax assets were forced into bankruptcy, creating an unexpected pitfall.

One day, Katsunori Nagai, Managing Director of Tokyo Marunouchi Bank and chairman of the Kanto Bankers Association, consulted Naoto over the phone, "The banking industry is in another serious situation–the 'bad debt problem' has simply turned into a 'deferred tax assets' problem. 'Tax effect accounting' was introduced as a trump card to quickly solve the bad debt problem, but now we're bleeding out in a different way. Where did we go wrong here?"

Naoto was surprised at the frantic energy in Nagai's voice, he had never seen the man bothered before. "The essence of this problem is the Ministry of Finance's excessive power. I believe the Ministry of Finance is having the accounting auditing industry create detailed interpretation guidelines on whether 'tax effect accounting' is being applied appropriately and creating an over-policing situation. In the first place, the Ministry of Finance is only supposed to provide guidance and ensure the capital adequacy ratio of banks does not fall below 8 percent. So it would've been sufficient to simply establish the calculation method. Instead, they threw the responsibility to the audit industry. It's an 'over-reach' and no one is sure what is allowed or not. The only solution is for the Ministry of Finance and the auditing industry to be held accountable for their respective roles, no more, no less."

Nagai must've had a burst of inspiration, yelling out, "Understood!" and hung up.

The buzz around the office the next day was that Nagai had stormed up to the Ministry building and demanded that they lessen the policing by the auditing firms. He demanded that calculating the capital adequacy ratio of the 'deferred tax assets' should be managed with a difference in creditworthiness.

After that, the banking industry focused on corporate revitalization and pivoted to solve this problem on its own, without the need of outside authorities intervening, to prevent the situation from ever occurring again.

Chapter 6　The Walls of the Ministry of Justice

When Naoto joined the bank in 1976, there were a total of 13 city banks. Now, they've consolidated into four groups–Inaho Group, Mitsukoshi Igeta Group, Marunouchi UBJ Group, and Risou Group. At that time, the seven major ones out of the thirteen were Daiichi Bank, Fuyo Bank, Igeta Bank, Mitsuwa Bank, Marunouchi Bank, Mitsukoshi Bank, and Toyo Bank. When each bank announced its financial results, they would individually hold an internal policy review meeting to compare with other banks and consider priority measures for the next fiscal year. However, these groups were limited to comparisons of the banks themselves, and did not include subsidiaries (with more than 50% investment by the parent company) and affiliated companies (with more than 20% investment by the parent company). This was allowed back then because the bank's share of the entire group was large enough to represent the entire group's strengths.

From 1989 to around 2019, Japanese companies aimed to expand their business scope and significantly increased their number of subsidiaries and affiliates. So it's no longer possible to use this method to truly understand the worth of the entire group with just an analysis of the bank. This led the industry to request that the Ministry of Justice lift the ban on holding companies that oversee the entire financial group. In June 1997, the Ministry finally took steps to revise the Antimonopoly Act, incorporating said lifting of the ban. As a result, the establishment of a 'holding company' to control the entire group was permitted, which had been prohibited for many years due to the dissolution of the zaibatsu financial conglomerates during US occupation. In light of these developments, the tax law also established a 'consolidated tax system' and compiled an organizational restructuring tax system to support group business management.

In 2002, the president of Tokyo Marunouchi Bank, Mr. Kishimoto, took the lead in turning to group management and was the first financial institution to incorporate the consolidated tax payment system. The company was quick to set up their own group management system with the holding company Marunouchi Tokyo Financial Group (MTFG) at the top. However, this also triggered a management integration with Marunouchi Trust and Marunouchi Banking.

The integration seemed smooth at first. However, right as the holding company's first period financial results were completed and dividends were about to be distributed to shareholders as planned, those in charge realized that the holding company did not have any 'retained earnings' to fund those dividends. The Commercial Code requires that dividend funds (profit available for distribution) be secured at the end of the previous fiscal year when paying dividends to shareholders for the purpose of 'protecting creditors'. The dividend source was limited to 'retained earnings', which is the accumulation of profits earned each year. The MTFG was newly established, so there was no profit to use.

The Commercial Code did not anticipate the newly emerging holding companies–the Ministry of Justice should have addressed this issue when revising the Antimonopoly Act.

Naoto represented the bank and immediately appealed directly to the Ministry of Justice. The person in charge of the Ministry of Justice at the time was Chief Murata. In the past, Naoto had had a heated argument with the man to get the tax effect accounting recognized under the Commercial Code, so the tension between them was not the best.

"Chief Murata, our holding company, and likely many others, is unable to pay dividends to shareholders in our first year of establishment due to the Commercial Code. The fact is that the Ministry of Justice neglected to respond when it lifted the ban on holding companies."

"You again?" The other man's decorum dropped once Naoto opened his mouth. "When we introduced the Tax Effect Accounting before, there was pressure from all sorts of big politicians in the Liberal People's Party, so we had to cut back. You're not going to luck out this time. The Ministry of Justice has already properly dealt with the issue. When a holding company is newly established, it is allowed to take over the profits of its subsidiaries as 'capital surplus', which is recognized as 'dividendable profits'. Therefore, even if there aren't any retained earnings, you can make do with that loophole. We won't consider it illegal."

Naoto had prepared for Murata to not easily admit their negligence, but the man countered with something already woven into the law. However, officials who were unaware of the actual practice of paying dividends wouldn't have questioned whether it would work in actual corporate activities. Naoto was stunned and couldn't close his mouth.

The Ministry of Justice was skilled in 'vertical administration'–as long as their ducks were in a row, it didn't matter what happened to other ministries. Murata should have been well aware of this issue, but it didn't seem to bother him.

"Go ahead and consult with the National Tax Agency!" was the last thing Murata offered.

As the Ministry of Justice argued, if the capital surplus was used for dividends, the tax treatment would be a 'refund of capital' for the dividend payer and a 'return of investment' for the shareholder. In other words, shareholders who invested would not receive dividends that could be recorded as profits as they had expected. In addition, not only could it not be recorded as profit, but if the price has fallen compared to the initial investment price, a loss would occur. It would end up being a surprise burden on the bank's business partners.

Yet Naoto had no chance of persuading the National Tax Agency. Instead, he temporarily gave up and reported the issue to President Shigeru Itsuki. As expected of top management, he was viewing this problem from a completely different angle. Perhaps based on his many years of experience, rather than dealing with the Ministry of Justice and the National Tax Agency, Itsuki decided that it would be better to clarify the negligence and appeal to investors out right that they cannot pay dividends this term.

Naoto immediately called the listing management office of the Tokyo Stock Exchange. "Tomorrow, could you make a press release regarding this term's dividend? The specific content is 'How government inaction is a hindrance to Japanese investment activities'." The news went out the next day.

Chapter 7 The Management Integration Battle

Even after the lost decade (1992-2002) after the bubble economy, the problem of non-performing loans showed no sign of abating. UBJ Bank, one of the major city banks, was teetering on the brink of bankruptcy. On August 20, 2003, the Financial Services Agency began a special inspection of a concentrated inspection of 100 large lending customers led by Chief Inspector Osaki. His first target was a major city bank in the Kansai area–Naoto later found out it had been Mitsukoshi Igeta Bank or UBJ (United Bank of Japan) Bank, which was created by merging Mitsuwa Bank and Toyo Bank. Both were so badly financially damaged that they could go bankrupt at any moment. On October 9th of the same year, the inspection team led by Chief Inspector Osaki laid siege to the Tokyo headquarters of Mitsukoshi Igeta Bank and UBJ Bank. The inspection had been scheduled for about two months then, but an employee from Toyo Bank had told the inspector under the table that there were double accounts of bad loans being covered up. As a result of the accusation, it became clear that Mitsuwa Bank had concealed the assessment materials of its customers. The investigation continued on until March of the following year.

On April 23, 2004, the Financial Services Agency announced the results of the inspection–a deficit of approximately 700 billion yen. In response to this, the top management of the bank decided to sell UBJ Trust and Banking to Igeta Trust and Bank for 300 billion yen in order to raise funds for the shortfall in reserves. It seems that the remaining 400 billion yen was planned for a public offering. However, on June 18th, the Financial Services Agency issued a business improvement order to UBJ Bank on the grounds of 'inspection evasion' (an act that interfered with the inspection). As a result, the top management of the bank was forced to abandon the planned public offering due to credit concerns.

In response to the business improvement order, the entire management team resigned, and the newly appointed president, Munetaka Okita, called up Shigeru Itsuki and asked for 'capital support'. Eventually, they reached a basic agreement with Igeta Trust and Banking. The memorandum to sell UBJ Trust Bank for 300 billion yen was withdrawn, and UBJ Bank was surrendered to Tokyo Marunouchi Bank. From there on, an unprecedented battle began between Tokyo Marunouchi Bank and Mitsukoshi Igeta Bank over the business integration with UBJ Bank.

Naoto hurriedly investigated the details of UBJ Bank's most recent assets and liabilities through their published financial statements. He found out the actual net assets of the bank (actual assets after deducting liabilities from assets and adding unrealized gains and losses) were in real excess of liabilities (debt exceeds assets) when the amount of public funds received was excluded. The Commercial Code prohibited business integration with companies who had excessive debt, it was a betrayal of trust to the shareholders. Naoto was asked by the president about the problem of insolvency and the merger ratio, and wondered what kind of reasoning could explain that UBJ Bank was not actually insolvent.

"UBJ Bank is actually insolvent, but judging by their outstanding sales capabilities, it can also be said that they aren't. However, that is premised on them generating that much profit after the management integration."

It was thought that everyone would be satisfied with that merger ratio, but on July 30, 2005, Mr. Higashikawa, the president of Mitsukoshi Igeta Bank, abruptly decided that the merger ratio should be one to one–a merger of equals with UBJ Bank. This proposal was so reckless that he was later called 'the madman' among his companions. The two banks took it as an opportunity to launch various countermeasures.

President Higashikawa's next move was a 'Tender Offer (TOB)' to acquire 51 percent of the outstanding shares of UBJ Bank. On September 10th of the same year, Tokyo Marunouchi Bank's President Itsuki decided to provide 700 billion yen in capital support to UBJ Bank. Furthermore, in order to prevent the ratio of acquired shares from being diluted, a takeover defense measure called a 'poison pill' (a poison pill clause grants existing shareholders the right to issue new shares in advance) was rolled out. As expected, President Higashikawa had no further moves, and on February 25, 2006, he formally announced that he would withdraw from the plan for the business integration with UBJ Bank. As a result, the merger ratio between Tokyo Marunouchi Bank and UBJ Bank went from 0.3 to 0.62, as initially calculated by Naoto, and the value of UBJ Bank more than doubled.

Perhaps President Higashikawa's strategy from the beginning was trying to create a disadvantage for Tokyo Marunouchi Bank's shareholders. Or conversely, did he mean to give profits to UBJ Bank's shareholders? Either way, soon after, the man decided to pursue a management integration with the Yamato Securities Group.

Witnessing such unprecedented negotiations, Naoto's view on the decorum for upper management was skewed. Was it okay for a manager to run a company based on personal stubbornness? It was the workers who worked under him who were always swayed by the orders of the top management. If it was just a personal rivalry, it would be a tremendous waste of management resources. Because in the meantime, the management crisis of UBJ Bank would continue to progress rapidly. Depending on the situation, they could have even gone bankrupt, going against everyone's interest.

Chapter 8 The Impatience of the Minister of Finance

Musashi Takeda served as the Minister for Financial Affairs for two years, from September 2002 to September 2004. He made use of his study abroad experience at Harvard University to forcefully proceed with the disposal of non-performing loans of Japanese banks after the collapse of the bubble economy. However, due to the rapid increase in bad loans in Japan during this period, it did not decrease according to his envisioned scenario. At Harvard, he studied the past methods of disposing of non-performing loans in the United States. So during his tenure in office, he formulated the 'financial revitalization program', commonly known as the 'Takeda plan', in order to achieve results, and forced major financial institutions to follow him. It was said that Tsuyoshi Motomura, a former Bank of Japan manager, supported this plan behind the scenes.

Specifically, financial institutions would be required to conduct strict asset assessments to determine the repayment potential of loans. These results would be reflected in international capital adequacy ratio regulations, resulting in a minimum capital adequacy ratio that had to be met. If it fell below 8%, it was possible to invoke a 'business improvement order' that would force the entire management to resign. Furthermore, as a numerical target, existing non-performing loans were supposed to be sold within two years, and newly occurring non-performing loans should be completely separated from the balance sheet within three years. Under the Takeda Plan, each financial institution's main business goal was to sell bad loans. The employees on the frontline had struggled with these operation policies handed down from headquarters to 'revitalize business partners with poor performance' so far. Yet, the business model that had been built up over many years had changed, and the relationship of trust between banks and customers had completely collapsed.

When Naoto accompanied President Itsuki on a visit to the Financial Services Agency, he heard a discussion between him and Minister Takeda. "Mr. Itsuki, when will Japanese financial institutions get serious about reducing bad debts? Japan is going to sink if this continues. Bank managers should be urgently removing bad loans from foreign financial institutions. Shouldn't you sell them to an agency and try to reduce it all at once?"

"I agree with what you're saying, but unlike Western banks, Japanese banks take a longer-term view of their relationships with their business partners. Unlike European and American banks, which simply cancel long-term transactions and sell those loans on the market, we regard the revitalization of our business partners as the most important management issue. I believe that will eventually lead to the revival of the Japanese economy."

"If you take such a passive stance, the bank itself may go bankrupt."

"Of course," President Itsuki defended, "we're advising clients with no prospects of revitalization to go bankrupt or close down their businesses, and then we work together with them to consider their best options. We aren't standing by doing nothing."

Minister Takeda was trying to introduce methods used by Western banks, but this was Japan and they would not necessarily fit. It would be more effective to have a unique Japanese way of thinking about revitalization along with each company, using the relationship that had been cultivated over many years.

At that time, President Itsuki urged Naoto to speak. Naoto thought it would be better to explain the differences in lending practices between Japan and the United States in order to get Minister Takeda, who was familiar most with the disposal of bad loans in the United States, to understand. "Minister, Japan's non-performing loans currently exceed 50 trillion yen and are continuing to increase. That's more than double the past peak level of non-performing loans in the United States. The major difference in terms of non-performing loans is that in the United States, direct financing is mainstream in the United States, and there is not as much dependence on bank loans (indirect financing) as there is in Japan. This may be because the level of dependence isn't high, and because lending practices differ greatly between Japan and the United States. In the United States, loans are made for individual projects (businesses), and Japan recognizes bad loans on a company-by-company basis. As a result, the rate that non-performing loans are increasing is overwhelmingly faster in Japan. Furthermore, in the U.S., project loans that have become non-performing loans can be sold in the market, but in Japan they are loans to business partners and can't simply be sold on the market. The Takeda Plan imposes targets for the major banks to sell non-performing loans. In that case, the banks will suffer further losses due to the fire sale at a discounted price, and lead to bankruptcy. So I think we'll stick with focusing on our business partners instead of this plan."

"Mr. Yamamoto, I suppose there's some truth to what you are saying, but if you look at the current crisis, that kind of response will be too slow."

The deadline for achieving the non-performing loan reduction target set by Minister Takeda was aligned with his own tenure, so there wasn't much time left. In the end, the Takeda Plan turned into a 'bankruptcy plan' that forced business partners with worsening business conditions to leave without question. This left the longstanding relationship of trust between banks and companies to crumble. It was a complete overthrow of the bank business model. Few people could say with certainty that the plan hadn't contributed to the current decline of the banking industry.

Chapter 9 The Obituary of an Old Enemy

On December 2nd, 2019, Naoto's nemesis from his banking days, Shunichi Osaki, former head inspector of the Financial Services Agency, died of lung cancer at seventy-two years old.

He had helped with the NYSE listing of Marunouchi Bank, the merger with Tokyo Nihonbashi Bank, the bad debt problem, the management integration with Marunouchi Trust and Banking, the establishment of a financial holding company, the rescue merger of UBJ Bank, the Lehman Shock, the Morgan Stanley crisis, and even more. He had been both an ally and a rival for Naoto. Even after Naoto retired from the bank, the fateful relationship continued. In fact, about a month before he died, Osaki called him up.

"Hey Naoto," he started, deciding they were on a first-name basis, "how are you? I'm in the hospital at the moment. I hope you're taking care of yourself as well. You're still caring for your wife?"

"Mr. Osaki, what happened to you all of a sudden? I heard you climbed up to the head of the inspection department, as expected. However, being hospitalized is not like you. Go ahead and take a slow recovery. We're not old enough to be old men yet."

"Yeah, it's calmed down at work, so I'm going to take a good rest. Though, recently, there are times when I feel strangely nostalgic for the old days. I thought about some of our own bouts and wanted to reminisce."

Naoto laughed. "What's wrong? I don't recognize this timid person? You're only 72 years old, aren't you? We're in an era where 100 year olds aren't uncommon. We still have nearly 30 years left." He tried to keep a light-hearted tone, but his smile faltered on his end of the phone. "So which hospital are you at? Maybe I'll swing by."

"I can't take up your time like that. Your wife's nursing care takes enough of your time. There's nothing I can do right now. I'll see you in Kasumigaseki when I get well again."

Naoto still couldn't shake the concern. Osaki wasn't the kind of weak person who called nostalgically for the old days. When Naoto heard the news of his death a little bit later, he regretted not visiting him at that time. That night, Naoto had a dream about Osaki. In the dream, he was in good spirits, but deeply regretful.

"Hey Naoto, I've been in the Ministry of Finance for nearly fifty years, and I have been in charge of the banking industry for more than half of that time. In order to solve the problem of bad loans, I risked my health for financial inspections. When

I was called by Minister of Finance Takeda to shake his hand and was encouraged to do my best for Japan, I had a sobering thought, 'If I don't do it, who else will?' However, after I met Naoto Yamamoto from Marunouchi Bank, my thoughts began to waver, wondering if this would really improve Japan. Because the more stringent my inspections were, the more banks went bankrupt, leaving the employees and their families must have been lost. I wondered if such a thing would really benefit Japan. On that point, you were thinking of a completely different solution to me, the corporate revitalization. I still wonder which one was correct."

In fact, Osaki had had a rival in the same examination department–Kozo Nakamura, who entered the ministry at the same time as him. Nakamura was a theorist and Osaki was a practitioner, and together they were the top two performers in the Financial Services Agency's inspection department. Osaki was promoted to the department manager first on the recommendation from Minister of Finance Takeda, but Nakamura was appointed as the department manager soon after that as Osaki's successor. In the end, this rivalry ended with Nakamura winning since Osaki died first.

Naoto was on good terms with Nakamura, since his bureaucratic way of life fit better than Osaki's idea of patriotism. In Naoto's dream, Osaki seemed to be driven by feelings of remorse, but if the problem of bad debt hadn't occurred, he would have taken a completely different life as an inspector. And that was true for Naoto as well. If it hadn't been for the bad debt problem, Naoto would have followed a completely different path as a banker. However, neither of them had any regrets about their lives so far. Unfortunately, Osaki may have passed away, but Naoto still had a lot of work to do. Naoto told Osaki in heaven. "Osaki-san, you've been indebted to me for a long time. History will prove your achievements someday. You weren't just a strong-armed inspector."

Epilogue Separation

April 29th, 2022 around 6 o'clock in the early morning, the first day of Golden Week, Naoto's cell phone rang. He fumbled for the device, wondering who was calling this early, but the line was dead when he answered. When he called back the number, a teller answered from the Motosumiyoshi branch.

"Oh Mr. Yamamoto," a female voice answered, "I'm sorry to be so early in the morning. Actually, my husband, Makoto Hiara, worked under you for a couple years. He passed away at noon yesterday from a ruptured aortic aneurysm. He suffered cardiopulmonary arrest in the ambulance on the way to the hospital, and was already dead when he arrived."

Naoto could tell from his wife's voice that she was crying on the other end of the phone. "That's terrible to hear! He was so healthy, he was only in his sixties, right? I can't believe it."

"Mr. Yamamoto, what should I do now? I don't even know who to contact at the bank about my husband's passing. Until now, my husband has been doing everything by himself. For the time being, I went to the bank to withdraw the money I needed immediately, but it seems he used fingerprint authentication, and I can't withdraw money with a card."

"Did the person in charge at the bank help you once you

explained?"

"Yes, but they claimed they couldn't do anything. It was upsetting to here from the place my husband had worked at for years."

"That must have been difficult. I'll take care of all of the funeral expenses, so please don't worry. Also, regarding the obituary, today is the first day of Golden Week, so I don't know how many people will see it. But I'll try calling everyone I know."

"I didn't even know who to call, but recently my husband and I were talking about you, so it was the first thing that came to mind."

"The funeral schedule has not been decided yet, right?"

"That's right. We don't know when the cremation will be possible due to the holidays, so the date has been decided."

"Okay. Please let me know when the funeral home gets back to you."

Hirata had joined Marunouchi Bank in 1982 and was first assigned to the Motosumiyoshi branch. He spent a year as a fixed deposit teller and soon after transferred to the loan division to replace Naoto. The younger man always had a chipper attitude. He was from Oita and attended the Faculty of Economics at Kyushu University. Sometimes, he mentioned being in the archery club during his college days, so Naoto contacted Hiratsuka, who had been in the same club years earlier. "Hello, it's Yamamoto. Thanks for the Udon noodles you gave me as a souvenir the other day. It's been a long time since I've had the chance to enjoy the nostalgic flavors of Nagasaki. By the way, you know an underclassman named Makoto Hirata from Kyushu University, right? Actually, he collapsed at the office yesterday afternoon and passed away. He had a ruptured aortic aneurysm."

"Oh man, I hadn't heard."

"His wife called me and said she didn't know what to do, so I'm contacting people he may have known. He was in the same archery club as you, do you happen to have a graduation list for the archery club?"

"Unfortunately, no, we were far apart in age, so he didn't overlap with me in college. I tried to invite him to join the bank's archery club a few times, but at the time he said he was too busy with work. I don't think he ever attended a reunion either."

"Okay, I'll do some research and let you know the details later."

Hirata joined Naoto in the planning department where he was assigned to the 'office streamlining promotion group' that cooperated with the sales force. He worked hard until late at night every day, always one of the last to leave. Naoto had promised him they would go out for a drink when things settled down, but they were both busy and in the end they couldn't keep their promise. Naoto worked with him for two years at the Motosumiyoshi branch and five years in the planning department, for a total of seven years. Naoto still vividly remembers that before Hirata got married, he came with his wife, who was his fiancée at the time, to the company housing in Musashikosugi to say hello. At that time, both of them were full of happiness and seemed to be so excited with their dreams for the future.

Naoto was the first to inform his former colleagues that Hirata had passed away. Most had been at home because of the national holiday. In the end, he was able to contact all of them, and more than ten people attended the funeral. He was most surprised by the people that didn't come. Most of his former coworkers made the excuse that they weren't very close to Hirata, and didn't even bother to ask about the funeral schedule. Of course, it was also during the pandemic, so not wanting to go to gatherings was understandable.

The wake was on May 5th, Children's Day, at the nearby Kirigaoka Funeral Hall. Hirata had been blessed with two children, a son and a daughter. Of the three people left behind, the eldest son kept a strong front, but his wife and eldest daughter couldn't hold back their tears at the wake. His death had been so sudden. The moment Naoto touched Hirata's cold forehead during his last farewell, he had a strange feeling that he was trying to say something to Naoto. It was like he was about to open his eyes and get up. That night, Naoto had a dream about working with him at the Motosumiyoshi branch. As usual, he turned and asked Naoto, "Mr. Yamamoto, is there anything I can help you with? If we finish up early we can go to the bar down the street."

"Actually, I'm sorry, but could you read over this lending request for approval and check if there is anything wrong?"

He looked over the request for approval for a while. "Mr. Yamamoto, does this customer really need this loan? Isn't this a loan that the bank asked the customer to borrow? How is it helping the customer?"

"I understand what you're saying. It may not necessarily be necessary right now, but since sales are growing this much, it should be necessary to increase working capital in the future."

"There's certainly no room for objection to that theory, but I really want to put the customer first. Banks should not take advantage of their superior position. I think it's wrong, that's all."

"You're right." Naoto hummed in the haze of his dream. "I really think so too."

After that, he and Hirata continued their discussion as usual at their favorite noodle stand. Naoto called it a night, but Hirata protested. "But we haven't finished talking yet. Let's go to my house."

"Okay, Hirata, if there's anything you want to talk about,

I'll stay out with you tonight. You can tell me anything."

Hirata sighed. "When I look back on my life so far, I have nothing to regret. I was blessed with my beloved wife and two children, and I couldn't have been happier. But there were still many things I wanted to learn from you. I would like to ask you for one last thing. If I were to pass away without being able to say my final goodbyes to my family, I'd like you to say a few words to the three of them. 'My life was short, but I have no regrets. We had a really happy life as a family. It may be difficult for all of you from now on, but I believe that the family love we have built together will be strong enough to overcome various hardships in the future. Thank you very much'."

"Hey, Hirata, you're seven years younger than me." Naoto scratched at his chin, shaken by his words. "Don't say those kinds of things. Your life is still ahead of you."

In his dream, Hirata silently listened to Naoto without arguing. Then he suddenly stood up. "It was nice knowing you." Then he left without turning around.

Naoto involuntarily tried to stop Hirata. "But you said we haven't finished talking yet. Where are you going in such a hurry? Come back. Let's go drink at another bar."

At that moment, Naoto woke up. "Thank you very much, Hirata. I'll see you in the next world."

Part 2
Nursing Care

Prologue Life Expectancy

Yoko's weight was 65 kilograms–she had gained 27 kilograms from her previous weight of 38 kilograms when she returned to Kawasaki and began nursing care at home. However, her body had become so rigid that she could not move her limbs on her own. She was unable to undergo treatment without massaging and stretching her extremities first. She couldn't even roll over on her own, her fingers were always clenched tightly and her toes were always flexed. She even lost the ability to speak at all. Her brain's frontal lobes had atrophied, and her cognitive function seemed to be mostly gone.

Naoto realized once again what it meant to be 'progressive' when Yoko could no longer do what she had been able to do when she was first admitted to Michinoeki Psychiatric Hospital in Nagasaki. At the beginning of her hospitalization, she was able to talk properly, and she clearly expressed her intentions. She went down to use the phone and repeatedly called her close friends for help.

"Hello, Mari? It's Yoko. I've been forced into a mental hospital by my husband. Can you contact the police and get me out of here?"

When Naoto heard about this from his friend, he thought it was a joke at first. But, when other friends told him the same thing, he realized she was serious. Eventually, when Naoto returned from the hospital to their apartment, there was immediately a call from Yoko, "Hurry up and get me out of the hospital."

While it had been rough, at least Yoko had been able to express her own intentions. Yoko would often talk about her food preferences on their way to and from the cafeteria in a wheelchair. "I prefer white bean paste to black bean paste for my lunchtime snack. Then I want to eat steak as soon as possible."

Naoto would often get her favorite meat dishes from a restaurant on the way to the hospital. However, Yoko's swallowing got worse within half a year, and she couldn't eat anything other than liquid food. She lost her voice. Every day, Naoto accompanied Yoko from nine in the morning until past five in the evening at the hospital. He did everything he could, including helping with her three meals, administering medicine, helping her use the toilet in her wheelchair, doing wheelchair exercises and walking, oral care, and massaging her stiff muscles.

Of course, they were mainly done by nurses, physical therapists, occupational therapists, and dental hygienists, but they only came three times a week. The only thing Naoto couldn't do was help her into the bath.

At this time, Naoto knew that the day would come when he would have to take care of her at home. When Yoko was admitted to Tozai Hospital for examination, Naoto asked her doctor, Jiro Asai, about the future.

"Doctor, as a result of a different detailed examination, it turned out that my wife's disease was not Parkinson's disease, but progressive supranuclear palsy. I was also told that there's no medicine that works for that disease. How long do you think my wife will have to live?"

Asai folded his arms and carefully chose his words as he answered. "Sir, what I'm going to tell you now is just general information, so please listen with that in mind. The average life expectancy for 'progressive supranuclear palsy' is considered to be 5 to 7 years after the onset. Of course, everyone varies. In addition, I think that most patients probably die from aspiration pneumonia. The atrophy of the throat muscles causes sputum and saliva. In any hospital, there's a shortage of nurses, and it is not possible to look after patients 24 hours a day, so if home care is possible, it would be the safest route. I think it would reduce the risk of pneumonia."

Naoto accepted that home care would extend life expectancy more than hospitalization. When she returned to Kawasaki and went to Sakuradamon Hospital, they heard similar things about her life expectancy from her doctor,

Saburo Sugiyama. However, three years had passed since then, and when Sugiyama saw Yoko being hospitalized that time around, he seemed surprised at how well she had recovered. It was probably because Yoko's weight had returned to normal and she looked like a different person than when she first went out. Naoto asked him the question once again.

"Doctor, my wife has regained her weight, and her blood tests show that her protein levels are within the normal range. Compared to worse days, her complexion and mood have improved significantly. Doctor Asai at Tozai Hospital in Nagasaki also told me that she would have five to seven years to live after the onset of symptoms, but seven years have already passed. What should we expect?"

Sugiyama spoke to Naoto with a troubled look on his face. "The next symptom that your wife will experience is probably respiratory failure, due to the progression of the muscle atrophy. There is not much time to decide whether or not to use a ventilator. She can stay alive with a ventilator, but once she puts it on, she can't take it off. Since she does not have the ability to make that decision, you as her husband will have to make it for her."

Naoto was quiet, looking between the doctor and Yoko. "I understand. I will take care not to trigger aspiration pneumonia as much as possible in home care, but it's difficult for me to decide on the ventilator by myself. I think I will discuss it with my family from here on."

Still, Naoto knew that their children would ultimately leave the decision up to him. He remembered something Yoko had said when she was still healthy. "If I can't eat anymore, I'd rather die. I don't want to be fed by a machine."

This is what Yoko said more than twenty years ago, and he had no idea what Yoko was thinking now that her cognitive function has disappeared. However, there was a clear difference between the Yoko hospitalized at Michi-no-Eki Hospital in Nagasaki and the Yoko now being cared for at home in Kawasaki. She used to have a painful expression saying, "Let me die already, please."

But now she has a calm expression. Naoto had decided to continue her home care regardless of what Yoko thought now. "Doctor, if the time ever comes when I have to put a ventilator on her, I agree to do it. But even then, I'll continue treating her at home."

Chapter 1 Rosary

At around 3:00 in the afternoon on August 10, 2022, Naoto's cell phone rang.

"Is this Mr. Yamamoto? It's been a while. It's Oda from the administrative office of Nagasaki Michi-no-Eki Hospital. How have you been? Has your wife progressed?"

"Oh, Mr. Oda. Thanks for your call. Both of us are doing the same. Is anything wrong?"

"Actually, I'm calling with sad news. Ms. Takano, your wife's roommate at the hospital, passed away. After your wife returned to Kawasaki, she had no one in rehabilitation with her. After that, her symptoms suddenly worsened and she became bedridden. Her swallowing function deteriorated, and she died of aspiration pneumonia the day before yesterday. As you know, Ms. Takano suffered from the same progressive supranuclear palsy as your wife. Her life ended just five years after being diagnosed. Her family members came to the hospital for the first time, and I was surprised to see so many of them. Tomorrow is the wake and the day after is the funeral. By the way, when I was cleaning up her hospital room yesterday, I found a rosary that was carefully stored in the back of her drawer. Under it was a sealed letter addressed to Yoko Yamamoto written on it."

"Huh? It's true that the two of them often went to rehab and rode the bikes together. When Ms. Takano finished cycling, which she loved, she always seemed to remember something, and immediately cried out, 'I want to go home, I want to go home'. At one point, Yoko placed an old white amulet that she received as a thank you when she was working as a shrine maiden into Ms. Takano's hand. Looking at it, Ms. Takano seemed to calm down a little and smiled at my wife. The rosary might've been a gift in return."

"I think so. I've heard that they were on good terms. With that in mind, I would like to send this to your wife. Is that alright with you?"

"Of course it's fine. By the way, was she a Christian? My wife went to a Catholic high school, Nagasaki Junshin High School, and it seems that she was baptized at that time. I think she took the name 'Diana'."

"I heard that she actually went to Nagasaki Junshin High School too."

"Yoko never mentioned that. I'll show it to her when she wakes up next."

"Thank you, I will send it tomorrow. I hope you're both staying safe during the lockdown."

Two days later, a large rosary arrived. When Yoko managed to open her eyes, her fingers moved slightly–it seemed like she remembered something. A while ago, on the way back from visiting her mother at the hospital, Yoko often stopped by the Catholic Church. At that time, Yoko would pray in the chapel with a rosary in her hand.

During the three years that Naoto accompanied and cared for Yoko, Ms. Takano never had family visiting. Maybe they had been hesitant to visit a psychiatric hospital. Or maybe it was because every time Naoto came, she would yell, 'Take me home'. In the first year, she often walked alone on the fifth floor. However, Naoto saw her halting in her path and suddenly retracing her steps. He was surprised to hear from Dr. Ueki that this was also a characteristic of this disease.

At that time, she had still been in alright physical condition. At that time, Naoto had no way of knowing whether Ms. Takano was married, or had children or siblings, or whether her parents were still alive. She suffered from the same disease as Yoko, and she was bedridden in the hospital until she died of aspiration pneumonia. She must have been unable to have nurses attend to her at every hour. If someone in her family had been able to take care of her at home, she could have lived a little longer. Naoto once again realized how home care could give patients great peace of mind. He also realized how many patients were dying in hospitals because they didn't have any available family.

Chapter 2 Gastrostomy Replacement

A 'gastrostomy' is a small hole for administering nutrients and medicines directly to the stomach. Naoto had witnessed this procedure when his father was bedridden due to cerebral infarction. After Yoko was admitted to Michi-no-Eki Hospital in Nagasaki, her swallowing function deteriorated rapidly, making it impossible for her to eat solid foods. Her weight was almost halved from 65 kilograms to 38 kilograms. Dr. Ueki strongly recommended the gastrostomy operation, and Naoto consented under the plan that Yoko would be at home in Kawasaki after. However, the gastrostomy device needed to be replaced every six months. Naoto and Yoko had been back in Kawasaki for half a year, so he went to Sakuradamon Hospital to make an appointment for the replacement surgery. Yoko's primary doctor was neurosurgeon, Dr. Sugiyama, but her gastrostomy surgery will be performed by a doctor of internal medicine named Kyoko Homma. After waiting for nearly an hour, Naoto was finally called to the examination room.

"Are you alone? What about your wife?"

"She's bedridden, and with the pandemic still in full force, I came alone today."

"That's fine. So what made you come in today?"

"I came to make an appointment for my wife's gastrostomy replacement surgery."

"This is the first replacement? Which hospital did you have it done initially in? How long has it been?"

"Yes. It was done in November last year in Nagasaki, so it's been about half a year."

Seeing the young doctor's way of speaking and the way she focused on the computer instead of looking at the patient's eyes, Naoto thought she wasn't on the same wavelength as him. It was not only because she was young, but also because he felt uncomfortable with her familiar way of speaking, as if they were friends. He wondered if that was simply how doctors were these days. Then she said something he could hardly believe.

"I'm busy, so I don't have a lot of time. When can you come in? I'm free next Friday morning. Can you come here next Friday at 10 o'clock?"

"Yes, that's fine."

"Then, please come to the emergency room next to the entrance on the first floor at that time. I'm going to have another surgery at one o'clock. Any questions?"

"How long will the surgery take?"

"About an hour."

"Okay. Thank you very much."

She's smart enough to be a doctor, but I don't think she's the type of doctor I'd respect.

On the day of, several nurses were bustling around, but when Naoto pushed Yoko's wheelchair into the treatment room while supporting her neck, no one moved to help them. They were completely ignored.

"Um, we came here to have a gastrostomy replacement surgery. My wife's name is Yoko Yamamoto."

One nurse replied with an annoyed look. "I understand, but we're busy with an emergency right now, so please wait in the waiting room over there. I'll contact the doctor."

Thirty minutes passed and no one came. Naoto was exhausted and found the nurse from earlier.

"I have been waiting for more than 30 minutes, but my wife is bedridden. So if it'll take more time, could you let her lie down on the bed in the treatment room?"

"Emergency patients are taking up most of our beds, so please wait a little longer."

In the end, Homma, the surgeon, did not come in until much later. Naoto took Yoko to the X-ray room in the basement, still in her wheelchair. The nurse who accompanied her kindly greeted Naoto and the others in the elevator.

"It's hard on you and your husband, isn't it? Has it been a long time? Please don't push yourself too hard."

Naoto was relieved that there were still good nurses at

this hospital. In the end, Homma performed the operation, but Naoto never got to ask her any questions. Six months later, the day came for her second gastrostomy replacement surgery. Naoto visited the hospital to make an appointment, just like last time. However, Dr. Homma was on a long vacation, so a middle-aged doctor named Masato Fujita took over instead. He came to say hello to Naoto and the others before and after the surgery. Naoto thought that was the ideal relationship between patients and doctors.

Six months had passed since then, and it was time to replace the gastrostomy for the third time. This time, Homma was in charge again, and her attitude was as unfriendly as ever.

"This time is the same as last time. Please come at 10 o'clock next Friday. Please finish administering her nutrients early, and her morning medicines are the same."

"Really? But last time the doctor said to not give her anything but a little of her medicine and only water."

"That's what Dr. Fujita said. I didn't say that. Are you misunderstanding anything?"

Naoto had no intention of arguing with her about such a thing, so he didn't pursue it any further. But the annoyance bubbling up didn't go away.

"The replacement surgery can be done with X-rays instead of using an endoscope, so today it will be completed in about 30 minutes. There's no need for general anesthesia, so it's not a burden on the patient."

"Doctor, this is the third time my wife has had a gastrostomy exchange. Both previous surgeries were performed under general anesthesia using an endoscope, right? Is it alright to do it this way instead?"

"It's up to the doctor to decide which way to operate at that time."

Naoto thought that she was refusing to admit her mistake. His eldest sister also received similar treatment at a hospital in Nagasaki. His sister developed what looked like hives on her hands and she died of a cerebral hemorrhage the same day she had a thorough examination for hospitalization. Her blood pressure had been a little high, so she was put on a blood-thinner. However, it ruptured a blood vessel in her brain, leaving her unmanageable. The husband refused to put her on life support. The doctor in charge and the head nurse at the hospital apparently gave his sister's husband various excuses instead of admitting it was a misdiagnosis. It wasn't difficult for the professionals to persuade a layman who has no knowledge of the disease that it was not their fault. The relationship between a doctor and a patient or patient's family would never be equal.

Chapter 3 Cluster Breakout

On Tuesday, March 8th, 2022, at two in the afternoon, Naoto gathered up children from single-mother households as he usually did through Kawasaki City's volunteer program, and helped them to study. It was a little before three o'clock when he arrived at the Musashi Kosugi volunteer site. The desks and chairs were lined up, and acrylic panels were installed to prevent spreading the coronavirus. By four o'clock, everything was ready. At that time, he received a phone call from the mother of one of the children. "Hello, this is Maeda Hiroki's mother. Hiroki developed a fever late last night, and when we went to the hospital this morning, it turned out to be COVID-19. He'll need to stay at home for ten days."

Four days later, on a Saturday morning, Naoto received a call on his cell from one of the project coordinators. "Hello, Mr. Yamamoto? Thank you for always helping with our volunteer activities. My name is Yamashita from the 'Asunaro-en' project. I apologize for calling so early, but have you had any changes in your physical condition recently? Actually, a volunteer contacted me earlier to say he tested positive for COVID-19. This person participated in the volunteer activity on March 8th with you. So, I'm currently checking on the volunteers who were participating in the activities that day."

"I'm fine at the moment, but I think there were five or six children participating that day. Are those kids okay? By the way, there should have been four adults too."

"So far everyone I've contacted has been fine."

"Oh, I see, that's good. So the volunteers who got the coronavirus were infected from somewhere else, I guess?"

However, around noon that day, Naoto began to feel something was wrong with his throat. He assumed it was allergies, but eventually he started feeling a little feverish. His temperature was indeed running high, not a symptom of pollen allergies. Naoto began to suspect he might have been infected with COVID-19 as well.

He hurriedly called Yamashita back to see if there were any other infected people, but no one answered. He reluctantly left a voicemail asking for a call back. Six hours later, he received a call from another volunteer, Tomita. "I'm sorry for the delay, we're a bit short-staffed."

"It's understandable. One of the volunteers told me this morning that someone had contracted COVID-19. I told her I felt fine, but then I had a sore throat and a slight fever, and thought I might have it. I called to see if there were any other positive tests among the volunteers and kids." Naoto coughed slightly. "I have a bedridden wife with an intractable disease with a low immune system, so if by any chance I am infected, it could be a big deal."

Tomita was silent on the other side of the phone for a while, seemingly hesitant. He then apologetically said, "Mr. Yamamoto, I am very sorry. To be honest, since we called you this morning, we learned that two children and one staff member who participated on March 8th were infected. We didn't mean to hide it, but I thought that making too much of a fuss would only increase everyone's anxiety. So far a total of 5 people have tested positive. If Mr. Yamamoto tests positive, it'll make 6."

"Either way the priority is to confirm whether I am positive. I will immediately contact my wife's visiting doctor and have her take a PCR test too. Thank you very much for calling late at night."

"Please let us know when you get the test results."

The next day, both Naoto and Yoko took a PCR test, and it turned out that only Naoto was positive. Although he was sick, Naoto was so relieved that Yoko wasn't any sicker. However, from there on, they were forced into multiple problems. Naoto was the primary caregiver for Yoko throughout the day, but now he couldn't have any contact with her.

Dr. Obayashi, the attending physician, said to Naoto, "Mr. Yamamoto, in hospitals and facilities, healthy nurses tend to positive-tested patients, but the opposite is rare. I think it's only a matter of time before your wife would get infected by you. I pray for a miracle."

After that, Naoto was prohibited from going out for 10 days, and Yoko, who was in close contact with him, had to be quarantined for 8 days. Therefore, Naoto had to take care of all of the services usually done by visiting physicians and workers, in addition to regular home care. He had to wear protective clothing and a heavy-duty mask to take care of Yoko. And in order to completely prevent infection, they had to identify the outbreak in their social cluster and take countermeasures.

Naoto first checked how many days' worth of milk and soy milk he had been using for Yoko's gastrostomy. He had enough stock of the original medical food for her gastrostomy for about a month, so there was no problem there, but the milk would only last two more days. Naoto rushed to the store wearing three masks and bought enough milk for the week and didn't realize until he got home that he had forgotten to buy food for himself. Instant noodles would have to suffice.

An even more serious problem was to take further measures to prevent Yoko from being infected during the next ten days of isolated home care. There was no contact from anyone in the volunteer group. Naoto began to think about how the upper management of Asunaro-en and the city of Kawasaki could properly recognize these critical situations and respond quicker.

In order to find out what kind of infection prevention

was most effective in home care, Naoto tried to find out what happened on the day he got infected. All communication with Tomita was done via email, so the timing was easy to keep track of. Though he stopped sending emails a few days prior, Naoto assumed it was because there was a lot of fuss in the park. Even so, Naoto did not let up on his pursuit of him, because without grasping the facts, the subsequent measures would be irrelevant. It gave him the same thrill as work used to, a challenging problem to take action to solve.

First, on March 8, a total of 12 people–6 children, 4 staff members, and 2 volunteers– were participating in the afterschool program. Of these, a total of six people–one child, three staff members, and the two volunteers–were found to be positive right after. Then the number of known infected people reached 10, including the family members of those originally infected. According to the definition announced by the Ministry of Health, Labor and Welfare, a 'cluster' was any group infection with a known contact history of five or more infected people from the same place. After reviewing all the information, Naoto had three questions. First, how did COVID-19 slip through the volunteer group's prevention measures? Everyone had their temperature checked at the door. Second, how did the virus get through even though everyone wore masks and frequently washed and disinfected their hands at least once every 30 minutes? Finally, there were 12 participants in all, but only half of them were infected with COVID-19, why?

It was clear that the cluster occurred at this venue, not from a community transmission. If so, they should be able to identify the first infected person. Two children had been absent from school two weeks before due to poor health–Hiroki and Yuuto. The two were good friends and always ran around the venue together.

Hiroki tested positive on the day of the event, so he did not participate. This likely meant Hiroki had infected Yuuto a few days earlier, and Yuuto came in before any symptoms showed, or he was asymptomatic. That may be how he slipped through the temperature check.

Now how did only one of the four employees not get infected? On the other hand, very few of the children were infected. In order to solve these two questions, it was necessary to examine the behavior of the participants on the day in detail. The only employee who wasn't infected must have acted differently than the other three. Naoto asked the female staff member who had not been infected with the virus about her activities that day.

"I always drop Momo off at her house at six o'clock in the evening. I was away from the venue for more than an hour that day."

Her time away probably prevented the airborne particles of the coronavirus filling the venue from reaching her as much.

However, Naoto's reasoning fell into a logical contradiction–
the five children who were not infected were at this venue the
whole time.

The actual development of symptoms, like a high fever and
sore throat, depends on how many droplets of the coronavirus is
ingested into the body. At that time, Naoto remembered he had
been playing a game with Yuuto for over an hour that required
the acrylic board being removed temporarily. The participants
were Yuuto, Naoto, and two adult employees, and all four of
them were infected. They had let their guard down since Yuuto
had been asymptomatic at the time. Therefore, ventilation was
the first decisive factor in preventing infection.

To survive this ten-day quarantine without infecting
Yoko, despite the chilly weather of early March, Naoto left all
of the windows open. Even when they went to bed, he turned
on the heater and left the window open. The measures were
successful, and Yoko remained uninfected. Dr. Obayashi, a
visiting doctor, was surprised and said to Naoto, "I was dubious
about you caring for your immune-deficient wife while sick,
but she seems to be fine."

It was a relief that the preventative measures had worked,
when used correctly. Sadly, the administration in charge of the
program was more concerned about covering up the outbreak
than preventing it in the future. Therefore, in order to sound the
alarm bells, Naoto appealed in writing to the concerned parties

to urgently implement better ventilation measures. Among them was an elderly male representative of the municipal housing complex they used for the venue.

He had received numerous complaints from residents due to the noise of children. In order to prevent further annoyance, he asked the staff to close all the windows, which may have ended up accelerating the spread of infection. With a full understanding of these circumstances, he made a request to the city of Kawasaki to install a large ventilation fan for commercial use in order to protect the elderly residents. When they seemed reluctant, he wondered if the government office thought the budget was more important than the lives of children and the elderly. The local government also stuck to a 'do nothing' principle.

The content disclosed by both parties to the citizens of Kawasaki speaks volumes. The important facts were concealed, and no real steps were taken.

[Information Disclosure from Asunaro-en]

"We have found that several staff members, children, and volunteers have tested positive for the coronavirus. We hope that those infected will recover as soon as possible. We will continue our work after considering infection prevention measures."

[Kawasaki City Information Disclosure]

"Regarding the occurrence of multiple positive cases

of COVID-19 among children and workers, we will work to ensure the stable implementation and enhancement of the volunteer project in cooperation with its people and related organizations."

He wondered what kind of excuses they would make when the second and third clusters occurred. No one seemed to think about the huge price inaction would take in the future, especially on children, the elderly, and the disabled. Shouldn't government agencies take these socially vulnerable people more seriously? The mayor of Kawasaki declared his own hypocritical slogan on their website as follows, 'Aiming for a Kawasaki City where children, the elderly, and the disabled can live safely and securely!' As a citizen of Kawasaki, he could only hope that this would not end up as a mere slogan.

Chapter 4 Allowance for Disabled Persons

On August 2nd, 2022, Yoko received a sealed letter from the Persons with Disabilities Support Section of the Kawasaki City Miyamae Ward Office. When Naoto opened it, there was a document titled 'Present Income Situation Report' which was carried out every year at that time.

'Regarding the Special Disability Allowance you are receiving, the payment will be restricted depending on the income status of the eligible recipient, his/her spouse, and the person responsible for support in the previous year. Please submit the following to the welfare office regarding the current situation and income status of said persons.

1. Notification period is August 12, 2020 to September 12, 2022

2. Reception hours are 9:00 a.m. to 4:00 p.m. at the Miyamae Ward Office, 4th Floor, 2nd and 3rd Conference Room

3. What to bring:
   · Documents required to confirm your 'My Number'
   · Documents stating the amount of public pension received by the qualified recipient from January to

December 2021'

His first impression when reading this document was whether the ward office had the authority to 'restrict special disability allowances'? Wasn't it extremely disrespectful to people with disabilities? On the website of the Ministry of Health, Labor and Welfare, the following information regarding special allowances for persons with disabilities was published, 'Relief of special mental and material burdens necessary for persons with severe disabilities who need special care in their daily lives. It aims to improve the welfare of said persons by providing allowances to help.'

In other words, special allowances for persons with disabilities were provided by the government, and the ward office was only responsible for the administrative work–the ward office itself did not have the authority to restrict it. In addition, even though they put, 'Please notify the welfare office,' in writing, there was no easy form to fill out and send. Instead, it requested that the person with disabilities either had someone physically go in their stead or get to a specific office on the fourth floor of a building. Furthermore, if people with disabilities are considered high-priority, shouldn't the venue be on the first floor? The mayor's slogan rang false again.

Naoto couldn't help but wonder how the whole situation seemed to be hindering disabled people instead of reaching out to help them. If he could ask the employees to change the wording in the letter, he would start with:

① "You are receiving" → "We are providing"

② "Payment will be restricted" → "Payment may be restricted"

③ "Please submit a notification" → "Please call the office"

④ "Documents required for confirmation of My Number" → "My Number card or its notification"

⑤ "Documents stating public pension amounts, etc." → "Not required" (My number card holders should be able to have their income ascertained at the government office).

On the day he had to drop off all of the documents, Naoto told the female receptionist at the venue, "I'm taking care of my wife at home, so I can't be out for long, if you could please take care of these as soon as possible."

"Please take a numbered ticket. I will call you when it's your turn, so please sit down and wait in the conference room," was all she replied with. Multiple people called him to different parts of the office, from one floor to another. Finally, he ended up on the fourth floor in the stated conference room to write down his social security information.

"You can go now." The man behind the desk dismissed him, shuffling the papers into a drawer.

Naoto couldn't keep down his irritation. "The government

office should be able to ascertain the income of anyone with a 'My Number' card, right?"

"I couldn't tell you myself, but you could contact my boss." He scribbled down a phone number, clearly wanting to end the conversation.

However, it was two weeks later before Naoto received a call back from said boss.

"It's difficult to explain over the phone, so first I'll send you the relevant papers to go over. After you're familiar with that, we can discuss it over the phone."

The documents never arrived, so Naoto had to call him and ask when the documents had been sent. Naoto couldn't trust his answer and told him, "If it doesn't arrive by the end of today, please deliver it to me in person tomorrow morning." As expected, it did not arrive that day. But, when he checked the mailbox the next morning, the papers were there. Naoto assumed the government employees would continue ignoring his calls, so in order to leave a papertrail, he created a written questionnaire and sent it to the government office by registered mail. The note asked for grounds for summoning people with disabilities in person. In fact, in the past, Naoto had submitted a letter of consent to the person in charge, saying that the government office could use his My Number to search for information, such as his income status.

What Naoto had hoped the reply would be was, "As Mr.

Yamamoto said, the Ministry of Health, Labor and Welfare will give due consideration to the circumstances of persons with disabilities, and if you have a My Number card, the government office will be able to tell you the income of the previous year. Therefore, there is no need for you to come next time. It was our mistake. I will write that in the notification form next time."

In reality, not only did they refuse to admit their mistakes, and Naoto's patience had run out. The office's explanation for Naoto's letter of inquiry was completely nonsense.

・Regarding the 'Special Child Rearing Allowance', which is the most common, we had moved it from the fourth conference room to the second conference room. → While this may have been true, all applicants drew a numbered ticket at the entrance of the fourth conference room and were made to wait in the conference room. At the entrance, no one checked whether they were applicants for that allowance, so it didn't matter.

・On the day of the meeting, the booth in the fourth conference room was full, but the second conference room was vacant, so in order to respond as quickly as possible, we moved to the second conference room to accept more people. → It wasn't that the second conference room was vacant, but that the second conference room hadn't been used from the beginning. If they wanted to respond as quickly as possible, people should be guided to both the second and fourth conference room to be dealt with at twice the speed.

・ We asked everyone to come to our office to confirm their address, bank account details, etc., as well as 'the status of admission to facilities, hospitals, etc.' If said person has been admitted or hospitalized for more than three months, you would not be eligible for payment. → Naoto never received such a question. He was simply told to write only his number.

None of the responses from them seemed at all sincere. It would take three or four more months to solve the problem. Why did something so simple take so long? Naoto, who was a businessman, could not understand at all. However, since Naoto has formally lodged a complaint with the Citizen's Ombudsman about the government's negligence, the government officials would hopefully make changes.

Chapter 5 Critical Home-Visit

Under the long-term care insurance system, elderly people aged 65 and over who required long-term care could receive the necessary care insurance services up to a certain limit each month, depending on the degree of care they need. Depending on your income, you would have to pay anywhere from 10 to 30 percent of the cost. Yoko had been certified at the highest level of need (so severe that she could not live without long-term care and was unable to communicate), so her monthly service usage limit was 36,217 units (1 unit being 10 yen). If the limit was exceeded, you would be responsible for the full cost of the excess.

In Yoko's case, she received a 'bathing visit' service four times a week, so her monthly nursing care service usage had already hit the upper limit. Naoto asked their government-assigned care manager if there was a way to receive additional care services. She made this suggestion, "There is a system called 'critical home-visit care'. If you use this, you can use a separate service from your current nursing care service. However, you would need to apply to the ward office and receive approval first. Unfortunately, I'm not allowed to be involved in this application, so you will be responsible for all the application procedures."

He went all the way to the Miyamae Ward Office first thing in the morning on March 2nd. He thought that by using this new system, Naoto would be able to go out for longer periods of time with someone watching Yoko. Naoto filled out the application on the spot and submitted it.

"Mr. Yamamoto," the person behind the desk started, "this application must be accompanied by a doctor's certificate. This month's review meeting is on March 28th, but in order to have it reviewed on that day, a copy of the application must be sent to the reviewers by the 5th. I think you'd have to wait until next month."

"Wait a minute. I'm in a hurry, so I'll go get a doctor's certificate by the end of today. Why do you have to send the application documents to the review committee by March 5, more than three weeks in advance? I can understand sending it to the judges in advance and having them look at it in terms of efficient operation of the judging committee, but why three weeks?"

"The jury members are busy people." The clerk shrugged.

"I see, so the government would rather give priority to the convenience of the examination committee rather than the disabled?"

"There's only two judges on the jury to handle the applications."

"And how many applications do you receive for this service each year?"

"Five or six cases a year," the man mumbled.

"Then, isn't there barely one case a month? Doesn't that make it unnecessary to send the application documents to have them look at it beforehand? Just consider them on the day of the screening meeting, isn't that enough?"

"No, no, this method has been in place for decades, so we can't just change it now."

"If the operational rules made by the government office do not match the actual situation, it's natural that the government office should change it. As long as you continue with those principles, nothing will get better no matter how long you wait. Who the hell are you working for if not the public? The residents here?"

In the end, they strongly resisted changing the conventional way of doing things. Then came the next problem. Naoto went directly to Yoko's attending physician to get a doctor's certificate, finally ensuring it would be examined at the examination committee that month. However, Naoto was surprised when he confirmed with the person in charge on March 28th, whether or not it had been approved. The one judge said that he went on a long vacation and only got back the day prior–so he probably had only looked at the application for the first time then. Naoto was waiting outside the office when the meeting finished at six in the evening–unfortunately, he was told that the result of the review would not be known until two days later.

"I'm in a big hurry though. I need to find a company that provides critical home-visit care and sign a contract as soon as possible. The application was sent in at the beginning of the month to have all the information pre-confirmed, why won't we know the results until two days later?"

Neither of the men could give him a clear answer–yet, he received a call from their higher-up that it had been approved. Naoto hurriedly searched online for any providers of home-visit nursing care for severely ill patients in Kawasaki City, and thankfully found that there were 22 companies. The first claimed they were short-staffed and couldn't accept new clients. In the end, he made inquiries to all 22 companies, but most of them replied that they had a labor shortage.

This government-provided system for severely ill people, would have been wonderful if it was actually functioning. The reasons were 'labor shortages' and 'aging of the caregivers themselves', meaning not enough younger people were entering the field to keep up with Japan's upside-down pyramid of population. This kind of nursing care was extremely risky for business operators, while the nursing care fees were probably lower than usual ones. The government wasn't doing enough to actually make it worthwhile for the businesses offering the program.

This irresponsible response of the government, which had previously gone to great lengths to establish a once-good system, was further proof of its inaction. The public servants seemed to understand the hypocrisy, but no one was trying to resolve it, letting disabled people and their families pay the price instead. Even at his age, Naoto still hadn't lived to see the world become a place where people with disabilities could live with peace of mind.

Chapter 6 Caregiver Rest and Respite Hospitalization

'Respite' means rest or relaxation, so 'respite hospitalization' referred to patients who were being cared for in order to prevent burnout for family members who are typically the caregivers. It was a system to temporarily hospitalize a patient, sort of like a short stay at a nursing home. Usually patients using this service had a hard time staying at a nursing home full-time previously. In other words, if a person required constant medical care, it was not called a 'short stay' in a facility, but a 'respite' for the caregivers to take care of themselves. On May 28th, 2022, Naoto unwillingly returned to Nagasaki for two nights to sell one of their rental houses. At that time, he didn't even know about the idea of respite hospitalization. So he asked their second son and his wife to take care of Yoko at home. He prepared detailed notes and taught his second son how to do it all while also taking care of himself several times in advance. There were no particular problems that time since it was a short stay.

However, on July 11th of the same year, Naoto had to appear in court with his sister-in-law, and he was forced to return to the city again. He also used this opportunity to visit some friends who were still active at the Education Foundation he had worked at and at the local bank branch.

At Yaso Bank, Ichiro Shinozawa, a fellow alumni from Nagasaki University, was active as a senior managing director in charge of finance, and he was also recruited as a member of the foundation. For some time now, Naoto had been appealing to local bank executives that unless regional banks are consolidated into one bank per prefecture to improve efficiency, they would sooner or later cease to exist. In order to do so, he explained that it was necessary to carefully consider establishing a holding company like Marunouchi Bank had done, and he explained several methods of business integration in advance. Killing two birds with one stone, he was also giving lectures about his experiences at Marunouchi Bank and recruiting members of the foundation.

Preparing for the trip, Naoto told the usual home-visit doctor, "It's been six years since her last major checkup, so it's about time to confirm any changes in her condition. Since I was advised that I should go back to Nagasaki, I asked Dr. Sugiyama of Sakuradamon Hospital for a temporary stay as a respite."

Naoto entrusted the detailed care instructions to the nurse in charge, but it seems that the hospital was not able to provide a proper log, as expected. First, her oral care was not available due to the lack of dental hygienists. In addition, no one was 'available' to dis-impact her bowels, supposedly due to the shortage of nurses–strong laxatives were used instead.

The next time Naoto had to return home to present his opinion in an upcoming trial, he asked a visiting nurse if there was any public system that would allow Yoko to be hospitalized for a short period of time. She finally told Naoto about Kawasaki's respite hospitalization system.

Naoto contacted the Kawasaki City Health and Welfare Bureau the next day. On the website, it was explained as follows:

"'Respite Temporary Hospitalization' allows elderly people who are highly dependent on medical care such as home oxygen therapy, tube feeding, artificial respiration, or intratracheal/oral suction. The purpose is to support the continuation of treatment at home by using the hospital when it becomes too difficult for those caregivers."

Then the woman in charge told him, "Mr. Yamamoto, 'Temporary hospitalization for safe watching' requires a lot of procedures and is quite troublesome. Rather than that, it would be quicker to ask your family hospital for a general short-term hospitalization."

Naoto hesitated. He wanted to be able to use this system, but she spoke in a discouraging tone. She continued to explain to Naoto, "Furthermore, under this system, the hospitals on duty to accept patients change every three months. Sakuradamon

Hospital, which you used for examination the other day, will be on duty this upcoming March. How about asking a hospital? Also, if you go through this system, it will be all private rooms, so the cost burden would be large."

"Huh? Is that so? When she was hospitalized for an examination the other day, I got a large room, but I didn't have to pay for the extra bed in a private room..."

"It's up to each hospital to decide whether to use private rooms or not. It seems that hospital management has become quite difficult recently, partly due to the impact of COVID-19."

Once again, Naoto was keenly aware of the absurdity of medical administration. "It's said that medicine is the art of benevolence, but how can we allow hospital management that disregards the patient and imposes an even greater financial burden on the patient and their family? There is something wrong there. When patients were young, they should have worked hard and contributed to the community. In the case of respite hospitalization, all of them are private rooms, and hospitals that collect the difference in bed charges. It's like it's saying, 'Don't go!' Isn't there something strange about a system that only wealthy people with income can use? Fixing this was the original role of the government."

Chapter 7 Hospitalization for Examination

On July 11, 2022, Yoko was hospitalized for the first time in six years. Last time she was hospitalized in Nagasaki, when her symptoms of Parkinson's disease were escalating too quickly. The detailed examination took three months. As a result, they found out that Yoko's disease was not 'Parkinson's disease' but 'progressive supranuclear palsy'. Parkinson's disease had movement-related symptoms, such as difficulty moving and tremors, due to a decrease in dopamine that transmits commands to the brain.

Progressive supranuclear palsy, like Parkinson's disease, developed in middle-aged and elderly people and progressed with symptoms similar to Parkinson's disease. However, it develops when the midbrain atrophies and an abnormal protein accumulates. The midbrain plays an important role in vertical eye movement, walking, and maintaining posture. Supranuclear palsy is named after the characteristic ocular movement caused by damage to the midbrain. The cause of the onset of both of these conditions varied, even though their symptoms often looked the same.

Both are diseases caused by mutations, but for Parkinson's

disease, the symptoms improve if the neurotransmitter dopamine is supplemented. For progressive supranuclear palsy it acted like Alzheimer's dementia, caused by brain atrophy.

Dr. Asai of Tozai Hospital in Nagasaki had told them, "There is currently no cure for 'progressive supranuclear palsy' and no medicine that works for it." However, he still recommended adding donepezil, a dementia drug, to the Parkinson's drugs, citing reports of improvement in symptoms. When Naoto heard him say that there was no other effective medication, he agreed. However, this drug called donepezil was a drug that turns the depression of dementia into a state of mania and it's said that it was dangerous to continue taking it for a long time.

However, Yoko had been taking donepezil for more than six years, albeit in small amounts. Two years ago, Naoto asked Dr. Obayashi whether it was necessary to review the medicine, but he said there was no need to change it for the time being.

At that time, Naoto didn't remember why he didn't investigate the dangers of continuing to take donepezil, but he once asked his local pharmacist, Yamada, the following question, "I heard that there's currently no medicine that works for 'progressive supranuclear palsy'. Nevertheless, my wife has been taking medicine that was originally said to be 'Parkinson's disease' for over six years. Is there really no problem with this? I'm worried about the side effects. But I just can't understand why a neurotransmitter replacement drug would work on midbrain atrophy?"

The pharmacist deliberately refrained from giving his own opinion, saying, "Pharmacists only dispense drugs based on the doctor's prescription, so I couldn't tell you."

Naoto thought that this newest hospitalization would resolve these questions, but he didn't receive any report of the test results done. It seems that the report was submitted by the attending physician to the care manager. In the first detailed examination six years ago, they took a blood flow test, heart sympathetic nerve test, head CT, X-rays, and DAT scan test to create a full image of the inside of the brain. A total of five atrophy tests were performed, but this time only blood tests and kidney/liver tests were performed, with no brain tests performed.

Naoto appealed to his doctor, Dr. Sugiyama, "I don't think Yoko, who is bedridden, needs a medicine that improves immobile legs and prevents falls."

If the patient's family doesn't study and check the reports seriously, would the hospital bother doing the proper tests? In any case, he was keenly aware of how difficult it was to administer medications for intractable diseases. Naoto visited the hospital to have all the tests done completely, and have the 'ventricular extrasystoles' pointed out in last year's electrocardiogram explained. When he asked my doctor and the attending physician at Sakuradamon Hospital again, they agreed to hospitalize Yoko for tests on the condition that she would be admitted to a private room.

When Naoto asked the hospital for an itemized bill, he was confused by the extra bed charge for her private room.

"The private room fee is 27,500 yen per night."

"No, just give us the cheapest private room."

"This is the cheapest price. The most expensive one costs over 50,000 yen."

If they spent 27,500 yen per night and were hospitalized for a week, they would have to pay the difference of nearly 200,000 yen for the extra bed. This was four months' worth of the 60,000 national pension. Naoto had been told by his doctor that a private room would be best for Yoko, who has an underlying medical condition during the pandemic.

After returning home, Naoto complained to himself, "In the first place, a private room at a hospital is standard if the patient wants to maintain their privacy, or for convenience, for showers and TVs."

Naoto tried to find out what was going on with Japan's medical administration on the Internet. It was explained on one page he found:

"Medical care in Japan is managed by public medical insurance. Almost all treatments, examinations, and surgeries received at hospitals and clinics are covered by health insurance. Furthermore, room charges are also covered by health insurance. If patients wish, they can be hospitalized in a private room, but in that case a special charge will be added to the basic hospitalization charge covered by health insurance. However, this is not necessary for the original treatment, examination, etc. Whether or not to use a private room depends on the individual circumstances, and of course health insurance does not apply, and the bed that is charged will not be covered. You will be responsible for the full cost."

Another page stated:

[Ministry of Health, Labor and Welfare Office Communication] June 24th, 2016 Health Care Notification No. 0624 No. 3. In providing a special treatment environment, we will provide patients with sufficient information and allow them to freely choose for themselves. This must be done with the consent of the patient.

○ Specific examples of cases where a patient should not be asked to pay a special fee for a special care room include the following.

(1) If consent has not been confirmed by the consent form

(2) Cases in which the patient is hospitalized in a special care environment room due to 'therapeutic needs' of the patient. For example:

· Emergency patients, postoperative patients, etc.,

who require rest due to serious medical conditions, or who are constantly monitored.

· Those who require timely and appropriate nursing care and assistance

· Patients with weakened immune systems who are at risk of contracting infectious diseases, etc.

(3) Cases in which the patient is hospitalized in a special care room due to the need for ward management, etc., and is not actually selected by the patient. With regard to institutions, there is a risk that patients' opportunities to see a doctor will be hindered, and it is recognized that this is unreasonable given the nature of medical institutions covered by insurance.

In other words, whether or not to use a private room is strictly up to the patient's own wishes, and the choice is left to the patient. In the Ministry of Health, Labor and Welfare's office communication, in order to prevent troubles related to the collection of the difference in bed charges from the patient side, there are three specific cases in which hospitals must not collect the difference in bed charges.

(1) If the patient's consent has not been confirmed in the consent form

(2) When there is a need for treatment, such as a weakened immune system or the risk of contracting an infectious disease

(3) When there is a need for ward management such as when the large room is full

In the final confirmation call, they were told to come at nine on the day of hospitalization for a PCR test, so they arrived at the hospital at 8:50. However, they were still told to wait for an hour. When they finally made it to the room, the staff said, "Only the patient herself can enter the examination room, so please wait outside."

"I'm sorry but my wife can't hold up her body on her own, even in the wheelchair."

"The nurses are too busy to provide that kind of support."

"Then who would take responsibility if my wife falls out of the wheelchair and gets hurt?"

As expected, the inspection staff were at a loss and seemed to have called the department in charge to ask for advice–how had this kind of case not been planned for in the first place. After thirty minutes of their deliberation, Naoto ended up accompanying Yoko to take the PCR test.

The receptionist handed Naoto a consent form for private hospitalization. Naoto said, "I'd like to request a large room instead…"

"I'm afraid they're all full."

"In that case, since it's a ward management problem on the hospital's side, there's no need for a consent form, right?

The Ministry of Health, Labor and Welfare's clerical contact certainly said so."

When he mentioned the contact from the Ministry of Health, Labor and Welfare, she grimaced and tried to go to her boss for advice, but Naoto wanted to put Yoko to bed as soon as possible. "My bedridden wife has been sitting in a wheelchair for more than two hours."

They were finally guided to room 302, a private room for 27,500 yen per night. Naoto then returned to the reception, but refused to sign the consent form for Yoko's private hospitalization, since the office communication stated, "the private room fee cannot be collected without a consent form."

Suddenly the communication lines at the hospital were quick when it was costing them money. Naoto received the call later that night, "Mr. Yamamoto, a large room near the nurse's station just happened to become available, so I'll move your wife there tomorrow. However, please understand that there will be an extra bed charge for a single room."

"I wanted a large room from the beginning, but I won't sign the consent form, even if it's only for one day."

The attending physician got frustrated. "Mr. Yamamoto, if you don't like our hospital, you can go to another one."

"Hospitals in Japan are funded by social insurance and taxes, and don't they carry out highly public projects that affect the lives of patients? Therefore, it's necessary to have competent authorities and the approval of the Ministry of Health, Labor and Welfare. We pay our health insurance premiums and taxes. We have the right to see a doctor."

"There has to be a relationship of trust between the hospital and the patient…"

"I'm not being arrogant here. It's just that I can't accept what the hospital says without any doubts. Shouldn't hospitals be more careful in providing accurate information to patients who are in such a vulnerable position?"

Naoto could not tolerate dishonest treatment from the hospital anymore. When he went to ask for an appointment to be hospitalized for testing, he confronted the doctor from the beginning, saying:

(1) There's a higher risk of being infected with the coronavirus in a large room

(2) She has an underlying disease that weakens her immune system

(3) She needs gastrostomy nutrition administration, suction for her sinuses, diaper changes, etc.

Due to the above requiring privacy, private hospitalization was still strongly recommended. It must be said that this was an act that clearly violates the administrative notice from the Ministry of Health, Labor and Welfare. Trying to collect the difference in bed charges without conveying accurate information to a socially vulnerable person like Yoko was not only a violation of office protocol, but also a despicable act that went against human morality. Japanese insurance and medical institutions were supposed to be operating on a highly public basis, funded by social insurance premiums and taxes. In the future, administrative agencies would need to closely monitor those dishonest hospitals. Medical administration that put the patient's needs at its center was required as soon as possible.

Epilogue Home-Visit Dental Treatment

As a result of Yoko's examination and hospitalization at Sakuradamon Hospital, Naoto received the following four explanations from the attending physician.

(1) Drug adjustment → In preparation for unforeseen side-effects, only one drug could be discontinued during this hospitalization.

(2) Echocardiography → Cardiac contraction was good with no particular abnormalities.

(3) Imaging examination of the head → As a result of the CT examination of the head, the atrophy of the frontal lobe had progressed more than the previous time.

(4) Dental visit → Although her oral hygiene was good, there was clear tooth decay.

During her oral care at home, Naoto had noticed Yoko's molars had slightly darkened, but it took a while to get a dentist appointment during the pandemic. When Yoko was hospitalized at Michinoeki Hospital in Nagasaki, a dentist came by at the hospital and had all of her cavities treated. However, there was no home-visit dental treatment for bedridden patients, so Naoto had to take Yoko to a dental clinic in another ward.

The hospital prohibited family members from moving hospitalized patients themselves, so they had to ask a nurse to carry Yoko in. Yet of course, they were understaffed and no one responded quickly enough. Naoto had to go to the dental clinic to make an appointment by himself. They got an appointment right away and he went to grab Yoko, but the receptionist told him, "Mr. Yamamoto, could you bring your wife in a wheelchair? A nurse from the hospital will need to support her during the treatment, so please have one available for about an hour."

When Naoto returned to the hospital room and told the chief nurse, she said, "Sir, I'm sorry, but the nurses have our hands full every day. We can't spare an hour to spend in the dental treatment room. If you really need support, ask an outside visiting nurse. Also, please don't make appointments for dental visits without our permission, to prevent this in the future."

Due to the shortage of nurses at this hospital, it seemed that nothing could be done without confirming the convenience of the nurses first. Naoto was stunned by this 'nurse first principle' under the pretense of a labor shortage, and replied, "Understood. Since the nurses are also understaffed, I'll carry my wife to the dental clinic. I will also support her for an hour during the treatment."

"I can't let you do that. We can't take responsibility if

anything happens."

"But I already got permission from the doctor to transfer her to a wheelchair and help her use the toilet in the hospital ward. How is it any different?"

Eventually, the nurse threw up her hands and let Naoto do whatever he wanted. At that time, Yoko hadn't had a gastrostomy yet, so Naoto took care of her mouth after every meal. At that time, she had only one decayed molar. But, there was a big fuss when Yoko bit the doctor's finger once.

Even after three years since she had the gastrostomy put in and returned to Kawasaki to start her home care, she still had teeth problems. Naoto wondered, "How did she get cavities even though she didn't eat anything from my mouth?"

The doctor explained, "The cause of tooth decay is the plaque that forms in our mouths. The acid produced by the bacteria that hides in the plaque causes the teeth to decay, and then dissolve. Even people like your wife who do not orally eat food have a lot of bacteria in their mouth. To some extent, the bacteria is removed, but not fully."

Naoto shook his head. "Yes, I understand, I suppose. By the way, during her hospital stay, they found a cavity, but why didn't they treat it while she was there? It would have been helpful…"

"Dental clinics at general hospitals have many outpatients as well as in-hospital patients, so I don't think any of them are doing home visits. Please ask for that home-visit dental practice."

When he contacted one of the dental clinics that offered it, the receptionist said that the dentist was currently outsourced and would not be able to contact him until next week. After being asked about Yoko's symptoms by another dental clinic, he was politely turned down on the grounds that she could not open her mouth and communicate."

Naoto was at a loss. Since Yoko couldn't say if she was in pain, he wanted her to see a doctor as soon as possible. Her decay would get worse and worse if she was left alone. At that time, Naoto remembered a speech pathologist who was in rehabilitation telling him about a certain dentist. "My husband, actually, he's a very devoted dentist who lives in Kanagawa."

The connection let him finally get an appointment the following Thursday. On that day, Naoto thought that the doctor would only check for cavities on the first visit, but he said that they should treat them immediately. It only took a little more than an hour to completely treat the two cavities.

There were still some splendid doctors who stood by their patients and secretly supported them and their families from behind the scenes. The Japanese medical industry hadn't given up yet. For the first time in a long time, Naoto felt relieved when he thought that these fine doctors were helping patients and their families in their times of need.

Part 3
Nostalgia

Prologue Alumni Association

On Friday, May 28, 2022, the reunion began at noon at Kouzanro at a restaurant in Nagasaki's Chinatown for Naoto's class from Nagasaki Municipal Minamioura Elementary School. At the beginning of the gathering, Chairman Saburo Tomiyama (affectionately known as 'Tomiyan') said that he had been preparing for this event until late the night before. He had downloaded the fanfare music from the Tokyo Olympics of their graduating year to his mobile phone, and planned an elaborate production where he would start the opening remarks right after playing it. However, no matter how many times he pressed the start button on the day of, no sound was coming out (later they found out it was in mute mode the whole time). The chairman stumbled over his words from the beginning, but it reminded them of the old days.

Following the chairman's address, Tsuguo Nakanose, who was said to be the most promising candidate for the next chairman, gave a 'cheers' to kick off the reunion. Of the 41 students in their class, three of them had passed away at a young age–Toshihiro Matsushima, Masakazu Ikei, and Tatsuro Himeyama. This reunion was planned by Naoto as the secretary, who had planned to return since everyone was celebrating their

70th birthday. Naoto returned to the city after spending two days selling the dilapidated rental house in Aioi Town that he had inherited from his mother. Naoto called on everyone to help hold a reunion, and finally recruited 15 participants to assist.

On the day of the event, Naoto greeted the attendees at the entrance of the venue, but after more than fifty years, there were almost no people whose names matched their faces. The first two people to appear at the venue were Yoshiro Makino, a dry cleaner, and Takashi Miyata, who then lived on his pension and had begun his hobby of ink painting in earnest. Since the two lived in the same town of Kawakami in Oura, they probably invited each other to come. When Naoto saw them, he recognized that they were classmates, but he couldn't place their names. He assumed one of them was Takashi Miyata, since the man had called earlier and said 'I'm an old man with a bald head and a protruding stomach, so you'll know me right away'."

When they approached, Miyata asked him, "Here, take off your mask and let me see your face. Yup, Naoto, I thought so!"

Naoto was surprised the man remembered his name. For nearly every participant, Naoto had to hesitantly ask for their names. The first woman to come was Miho Kuroi, who still had youthful energy, and Tsuyako Torisu, who had a distinctive snaggletooth. They came early because Naoto had asked them to host the banquet the day before. After the toast was over, those two beautiful people went around to pour drinks for everyone, as Naoto had asked.

As soon as they all had a drink in their hands, everyone was transported back in time, and old stories were blooming everywhere. It didn't take long to fill in the long gap of over fifty years. This was actually the third reunion for this class. The first one was seven years after graduating from elementary school, and it was the year when everyone celebrated their coming-of-age ceremony at 20 years old. It was the first time they all could legally drink.

Naoto no longer remembered the details of the first one, but for some reason he remembered the second party very well. The venue was the pub 'Jumbo' in Maruyama, which used to be a red-light district in the past, but was then a busy night district. Naoto, who drank alcohol for the first time at that class reunion right after he turned 20, didn't know his limit yet, and drank some gin and tonic. The rest of the night was a blur.

The next day, Tomiyan and Matsushima, who were together at the after-party, asked him, "Naoto, at the party last night, you were hitting on Miho the whole time."

"I don't remember much, did I really do that?"

After the second party, Naoto and Tomiyan took Miho to her home in Aioi-cho. Seeing the route to her house, Naoto's memory came flooding back. He remembered Miho's father was standing at the entrance of her house the night before, waiting for his daughter's return. Miho's father scolded the two of them so much that they suddenly sobered up.

"What time do you think it is?" They had no choice but to humble themselves and bow their heads to apologize.

The next class reunion was held 22 years later, when everyone was around 42 years old. The rumor was that Toshihiro Matsushima, a manager at Takeshita Electric Industrial Co., Ltd. in Fukuoka, begged the chairman, Tomiyan, to hold the alumni reunion that year. However, in the end, he was not able to participate in the second class reunion he had been looking forward to so much. His life ended at the young age of forty-two–the cause of death was heart failure due to overwork. The so-called 'sudden death'.

Around the same time, Naoto's chronic arrhythmia worsened, and he was told by his doctor to be hospitalized for treatment, and he was unable to attend the second class reunion as well. The age of forty-two was an unlucky time. Matsushima probably foresaw his own death and wanted to reminisce–he may have been desperately battling his illness.

Naoto was unable to attend his funeral, so six months later he visited the man's parents' home in Nagasaki. It was really hard for him to see his mother, still exhausted. He was painfully reminded of a mother's heartache at the loss of her only son. When he thought back on his own children playing with their mom, knowing the thorny path they would have to walk soon, he could not hold back his tears.

So for the latest reunion, Naoto had been at a loss at how to let everyone know about the reunion. The elementary school graduation album had the contact information of the teachers, but there was no address or contact information for the students–even then, it probably would be outdated. When he was at a loss, he remembered that there was contact information in the commemorative pamphlet from the last reunion. When Naoto found it in an unopened package that he had sent back to Kawasaki from Nagasaki, he tried calling up the numbers. However, when he tried the landlines listed, most of them gave an automated voice saying, "This phone is currently out of service." So he had no choice but to send a letter to the listed addresses.

During Yoko's home care in Kawasaki, he created a nursing care record to keep their children in the loop during the pandemic quarantine. He decided to include it and some other notes as his 'recent news' along with the invitation to the alumni. However, this little package caused unexpected trouble. A few days later, Naoto's cell phone rang while he was on the bus on his way to a volunteer activity.

"Hey, this is Kondo. This book was sent to me earlier, but I don't remember ordering it! What the hell is this?"

Naoto assumed that this Kondo was a senior at his bank, but the man was even more confused.

"No. This is Hideo Kondo."

"I'm sorry, this is Naoto Yamamoto, from Minamioura Elementary School."

"Eh? Naoto? I forgot about you."

Finally, the conversation between the two of them came together. Until the previous month, Hideo was in Libya, cooking for the Japanese government launching a large-scale project there to support developing countries. He said that he was now back in Nagasaki as a chef. He said he couldn't stay out late at night because he had to go to the market early in the morning for ingredients, but when I told him it was a daytime reunion, he agreed to participate.

Apparently, when he told his wife that he was going to Libya, she packed up his things and sent him back to his parents' house. So he was currently living a carefree single life. Several times a week, he would volunteer to teach people with disabilities how to work at a factory in Fukahori. As Naoto listened to Hideo's story, he couldn't imagine this was the same person he once knew.

"The mischievous Hideo, who was always grinning and restless, is now a first-class chef and actively participates in volunteer activities. What made you grow up so much?"

Another problem came from Takashi Miyata. The mail

Naoto had posted a few days ago was returned to Naoto with the other man's signature and seal saying, "I refuse to receive this." Takashi had returned the letter pack without opening it.

Naoto held his head. He underestimated how much fifty years would change a person. Maybe the man didn't remember the name Naoto Yamamoto anymore. He may have assumed it was junk mail. Naoto wanted to somehow clear up the misunderstanding. So, he took out this year's New Year's postcards, wrote the following in large letters: "I'm Naoto Yamamoto, a classmate from Minamioura Elementary School. I'm sending you a package, so please open it this time!"

Three days later, Naoto received a call from Takashi's cell phone. "I'm so sorry for the other day. I had just been discharged from the hospital that day. I had an operation to remove a kidney stone, and my doctor prescribed painkillers. But I forgot about them, and it hurt so much that I thought I was going to die. I was so irritated that I must have declined the mail."

"It's no problem, everyone gets like that when they're sick. I understand. I'll definitely send you an invitation to the next class reunion, for now please recuperate."

When Naoto was about to hang up the phone after saying that, Takashi hurriedly cut in, "No, no, I'll go to the class reunion! I may not be able to drink alcohol, but if I miss this time, I don't know when I'd be able to see everyone again.

I'll definitely go. Yoshiro Makino is also coming, right? Yoshiro had a mild stroke last year and was in the hospital for about a month. He worked hard after that, and thanks to his rehabilitation, he made a spectacular recovery. I must emulate his strength of mind."

"Well, we've all had a hard time. Actually, when I moved to Nagasaki six years ago, I had two heart surgeries at the municipal hospital. My heart convulsed and my pulse quickened. I developed atrial fibrillation. Thank you for your help. We've joined the ranks of the elderly, and we're all covered in wounds."

It seems that everyone read Naoto's recent news enclosed with the invitation to the alumni association. Everyone seemed to be looking forward to attending the reunion.

One of the friends he had contacted, Takeki, lived in Chiba Prefecture and seemed to be still single. He'd always been a quiet guy, and he still was. While catching up with him, Naoto began to think that he was suffering from some kind of mental illness. For some reason, he was unimpressed even when they talked about the good old days. Naoto couldn't convince him to come to the reunion, but before he hung up he said, "Takeki, you seem to be in a bit of trouble, feel free to contact me anytime. Kawasaki and Chiba aren't that far apart, so I'll come to you anytime. See you soon."

On the other hand, his old friend, Iwao, was the same

talkative man he always was. When he was in elementary school, his family of four lived near a park in Matsugae-machi. Naoto remembered visiting his house a lot. His mother seemed to work at night, and slept upstairs during the day. The kind-hearted Iwao would warn Naoto over and over, "Your voice is too loud. Mom is sleeping upstairs, so be quiet!"

He used to be a gentle boy because he was raised among his mother and sisters, but when Naoto met him again, his personality had changed so much that he wondered where his kindness had gone. He had become a selfish person who only made jokes and boasted about his triumphs.

"You must have had a lot of troubles since then too," Naoto said softly to Iwao, but the other man just laughed.

Emily Takayama returned to Nagasaki by express bus, and Asako Ueda came by plane–both of them were as charming as ever. Emily had become a little smarter, and had the aura of a lady who had aged elegantly. On the other hand, Asako had always been an active and open-minded girl, and still retained her cheerfulness and laughed merrily.

Naoto smiled at the sight of the two still friends. In addition, Kiyoko Homma, who lived in Oseto, a little far from Nagasaki city, remained youthful to that day. Everyone recognized her right away. She was a good mother of three children and a good grandmother to her grandchildren.

It saddened his heart to see how many friends he

had contacted that were unable to participate due to prior appointments or poor health. One had worsening chronic asthma, another had to go to work even on the holidays, and another was taking care of her mother-in-law. Three more were hospitalized. In this way, the reunion of around 15 people in total ended without incident. As Naoto returned to the hotel after the class reunion ended, he wondered, "Why was this class reunion, the first in more than fifty years, the most lively one?"

After all, it was the nostalgia for the innocent days of their youth, when there were no worries and a warm family watched over them, and their only job was to play. There is no other reunion that was as nostalgic and fun as the one for elementary school. Naoto prayed in his heart that night, "Everyone, let's meet again at the next class reunion! Until then, please stay healthy!"

Chapter 1 Absurdity

Naoto was born on February 10, 1953, by a midwife who ran a teahouse next to Doza Market in Nagasaki. Only eight years had passed since the end of the Pacific War, and he and his family were forced to live in poverty. His father opened 'Yamamoto barber shop' along where the streetcar line ran. The area was called 'harmonica alley' because the many tiny buildings were crowded together in a narrow alley, just like the finely divided mouthpiece of a harmonica.

His mother used her experience working at the former Mitsukoshi Bank to handle the accounting for the barbershop. She also had chores and other odd jobs, one of which was to recruit young employees.

"Young people wanted! No experience required, preferential salary, live-in possible."

It seems that applicants flooded in after hearing the advertisement–his mother had an uncanny ability to win people's hearts. Five people were selected from among the applicants, and then three of them were hired. At noon everyday, the three craftsmen would take turns eating lunch made by his mother in a small room on the second floor. He didn't know how his mother made lunch every day, squeezing in the time to go shopping at Doza Market between her barbershop duties. Naoto was well taken care of with the craftsmen taking turns coming upstairs.

Two years later, the number of regular customers had gradually increased. At that time, a thin middle-aged woman named 'Katsuko', the niece of Kame Yamamoto, his father's adoptive mother, came to visit. The Yamamoto family had a laundry shop with a boy of Naoto's age, Zentaro, as the heir from the main family, while his father was in the branch family. Despite being similar in age, Zentaro had a better physique, and Naoto always stood up to him like an older brother.

"I actually have a favor to ask of you. Originally, I thought I should ask Zentaro from the main family, but he tends to act too…haughty. That's why I'm asking you. Could you hire my eldest son, Makoto, here? After graduating from junior high school, Makoto fell in with the local delinquents. He doesn't have a job, so he plays around every day. Could he come in as an apprentice?"

My father had already hired three craftsmen, so he was at a loss and remained silent. At that time, his mother, who was listening to Katsuko's story from the sidelines.

"Honey, isn't it fine? You've been so busy lately, and you said you wanted to hire another craftsman."

"That's right." He finally nodded. "Shall we add another person? You guys can live here."

"Huh? Is that really okay? If we're live-ins, it would be hard to kick us out."

His mother was good at subtly suggesting her own ideas to his father, even as he stood up for her, and eventually making it seem like his father's idea. This was his mother's usual tactic of guidance.

However, one day, about two months later, two tough-looking men entered the barber shop. "Hey, Makoto. What the hell are you doing in a place like this?"

My father, who knew judo and kendo, told them to leave the store. While the three of them were arguing, my mother appeared and asked a middle-aged man who had come to the store for the first time, "Keiji, please arrest these two thugs for obstructing business."

The customer stood up from his chair and glared at the two thugs. Then the two of them ran away at full speed, thinking that this customer was a real detective. His mother politely thanked the customer, "Thank you very much, branch manager."

"No problem, you sounded like you were in a bind."

Later, when his father asked what kind of relationship she had with that customer, she said, "He's the branch manager of Yaso Bank, I do business with him every week."

His father burst into laughter. Unfortunately, Makoto disappeared from the barbershop the next day. A few days later,

Katsuko came to apologize to his father over and over again for Makoto's disappearance. All she could do was bring along and boast about her second son, who was a solid and hardworking man. His mother met this son and his wife for the first time that night. When she met them a dozen years later, they were both completely changed.

It all started with a phone call from the Togitsu Police Station. The two were involved in a local yakuza fight and had been murdered. Since Katsuko had already passed away two years earlier, a police officer at the Togitsu Police Station, who was at a loss to know their identity, found the contact information for 'Yamamoto Barbershop' in the son's amulet. The policeman asked Naoto's father to check the two bodies as soon as possible. His father was too busy with work to go, so his mother went to the police station instead. She was worried whether she would be able to recognize their faces when she had only met them once, but when she went there, she recognized them instantly.

They were cremated and laid in the same grave as Katsuko. His mother finished their burial and was surprised to see inscribed on the tombstone, 'Makoto Yamamoto passed away at the age of 24'.

Naoto would often play at the nearby Inari Shrine after returning from elementary school, usually sumo wrestling with the other local kids. He still remembers times when Makoto picked him up after dark instead of his mother.

At the Inari Shrine, the children of Doza Town would gather together to play after school. When the bell rang at five o'clock in the evening, mothers came to pick up their children. It seemed that Naoto's mother couldn't pick him up because the barber shop was so busy, so she sent Makoto in her stead. When Makoto went to pick Naoto up, they wrestled with Naoto for a while, like they were siblings. Naoto always went home on his shoulders.

Naoto had a dream of Makoto that night, after his mother informed him that he had died so soon after quitting the barbershop. He called out to Naoto as usual.

"Naoto, it's time to eat. How long are you going to play here alone? Your mom will be mad."

"Let's wrestle again! This time I'll win."

"OK, but this is the last time," Makoto said with a gentle smile as he spread his arms out to catch Naoto.

Chapter 2 Kindergarten

When Naoto turned five years old, he went to Teramachi's kindergarten, a different one than his two older sisters. At that time, there were about 30 children at his kindergarten. Among them were Shunsuke Matsuzawa and Goro Masukawa, whom Naoto later reunited with at Nagasaki Minami High School.

Matsuzawa's father ran a seafood shop in Doza Market and was a regular customer at the Yamamoto Barber Shop. The Masukawa family ran a liquor store in Atago. At Nagasaki Minami High School, Matsuzawa joined the rugby club and Masukawa joined the basketball club with Naoto. There were many other friends in his class that ran business in the town. The family of Naoto's best childhood friend, Kaoru Ayanokoji, ran the nearby public bathhouse 'Aya no Yu'.

Before his mother enrolled Naoto in kindergarten, she took him to visit and see if he could handle kindergarten alone. Once he was in, his mother came to the kindergarten for his entrance ceremony, but after that she never visited because the barber shop was busy. At his kindergarten sports day, his teacher, Mrs. Ohno, came to see Naoto eating alone. The barber shop was the busiest on Sundays, when the sports day was held, so his parents couldn't come.

In addition, Mrs. Ohno chose Naoto, who still could not read, to play the leading role in the play 'The White Rabbit of Inaba' performed by the kindergarten class on a local radio station. Since his parents were too busy at work, Mrs. Ohno taught Naoto one-on-one how to read and write instead. His best friend, Kaoru, played the main role of the rabbit, and subtly helped illiterate Naoto behind the scenes.

However, one winter day, a candle started a fire at the kindergarten, and the children's classrooms burned down. Everyone gathered at the main hall of the local Buddhist temple to listen to stories from the chief priest. At first, the kindergarteners were surprised to see the various Buddha statues and gorgeous decorations, so they sat obediently on their knees with solemn faces and listened to the chief priest's story. After a while, the children started running around and making noise when the novelty wore out. The chief priest, who was silently laughing at first, grew angry, perhaps because he had reached the high limit of his patience.

"Everyone, sit down properly. Any naughty children will be caught and dragged into Hell." At that time, the director actually jumped out in disguise as a demon. The children scattered and shrieked, "I'll be good, don't take me to hell!"

Naoto was curious instead and tugged on the 'demon's' robe. "But demons only take bad people to hell, right?"

The chief priest chuckled and asked Naoto, who the

teacher had mentioned still couldn't read, "Yamamoto, I hear you can't read yet. Can I show you how to read the characters written next to that Buddha statue?"

At that time, Naoto, who was supposed to be illiterate, saw it and said, "Namu Amida Butsu."

The priest asked Naoto in surprise, "How do you know how to read those characters? Who taught you?"

"Namu means 'to bow'. And 'Amida Butsu' means Buddha, right?"

The chief priest was surprised that Naoto even knew the meaning of the characters. Namu Amida Butsu was a common sutra recited by a monk of the 'Jodo Shinshu Otani School', which was the religious sect of Naoto's family.

The principal whispered over to the chief priest, "This kid must have been a monk in his previous life."

None of the adults knew who had taught Naoto that. He also liked all of the paintings of ghosts, and would tell stories about them to his mother, Aiko. "This ghost is a good ghost, but that one is bad."

Aiko asked Naoto, "How do you know the difference between good ghosts and bad ghosts?"

Naoto replied matter-of-factly, "Because good ghosts have kind eyes. Bad ghosts have scary eyes."

When Naoto turned seven, he transferred to Maya Elementary School, which had a long history and was in the middle of the city. At that time, he remembered that Maya Elementary School had just celebrated its 100th anniversary. His homeroom teacher was Masao Ito, whose name often appeared in textbooks as a contributor. His childhood friend Kaoru Ayanokoji was also placed in the same class. The two often went to school together because their houses were so close, but Naoto, who always got up early, had to knock on Kaoru's door, who was always oversleeping. Both of them were good at running, and had been representatives of the local relay team since they were in the first grade. The two were such good friends, but when Naoto was in the fifth grade, his father fell ill and closed the barber shop, so he had to move and part ways with Kaoru. The two would meet again in Fukuoka after becoming functional members of society; but that would take another 15 years.

Chapter 3 Anti-war Rally

In May 1963, Naoto transferred elementary schools. He was told to say goodbye to everyone after class on his last day. Naoto didn't know what to say, and while he was lost in thought, the teacher scolded him.

"Naoto, today will be your last day, but you were bullying girls until the very end. Kuniko Oyanagi told me the whole story. I'm asking you to apologize properly before you leave."

Naoto didn't quite understand what the teacher was saying. All he knew was that Kuniko Oyanagi told the teacher something, but why did she only believe her?

At that time, Kaoru Ayanokoji raised his hand and stuck up for Naoto. "Teacher, who exactly did Yamamoto supposedly bully? What if he was the one being bullied?"

In his mind, Naoto was silently applauding Kaoru. The teacher frowned. "Naoto, you always bully girls, don't you? This hasn't been the first time it's been mentioned."

Naoto gave a clear answer, "I'm not bullying anyone. Why would I bully a girl?"

The teacher was also annoyed by Naoto's cheeky remarks and addressed the whole class, "Well then, I have a question for everyone. If you saw Yamamoto bullying a girl today, please raise your hand."

Everyone knew it was all nonsense. There was silence in the classroom for a moment. Naoto said to the teacher, "You tell us not to suspect people without evidence. So, that's proof, I'm innocent."

In fact, the incident that sparked the rumor all started with the color of the cardigan that Naoto wore that morning. His mother had been so busy with work that she did the laundry late the night before, and the sweater Naoto planned to wear today wasn't dry yet. His mother reluctantly told Naoto to wear her sister's cardigan instead. Naoto hesitated for a moment at the sight of his sister's red cardigan. But there was no other option.

However, as soon as he entered the classroom, Kuniko Oyanagi saw his clothes and started making fun of him. "Naoto, when did you become Naoko Yamamoto?"

Naoto ignored her. Then she took Naoto's hat next and said, "I'll make this red too to match."

Naoto couldn't stand this and chased after her to get her hat back. At that time, she caught her foot on the desk and fell down. She cried aloud, "Naoto tripped me!" The problem was most of the class had seen her trip herself. Contrary to expectations, the teacher was surprised that no one raised their hand, but sensing the change in her favor, she changed the subject to Naoto's final greetings.

However, Naoto's feelings did not subside. Naoto thought that he should get a proper apology for her suspicions. "Today is my last day at Maya Elementary School, but I don't have any words to say goodbye to everyone. I can meet you all again anytime. But I think this will be my last time seeing the teacher, so I just wanted to say thank you very much for your help until the very end."

The teacher couldn't hold back their anger at Naoto's cheeky attitude, their face twisted in a scowl. At that time, Kaoru said goodbye to him, "Naoto, let's meet again someday. Then let's grow up together so we can laugh about what happened today."

Then everyone gave Naoto and Kaoru a big round of applause. On May 10th, 1963, Naoto transferred to Minamioura Elementary School. It had a peaceful atmosphere that was completely different from his previous school. Everyone was bright and the classroom was full of laughter–he was welcomed by everyone in the class. During the second period of calligraphy, Naoto neatly wrote the word 'hope' for the task.

Then Saburo Tomiyama, aka 'Tomiyan', who was like the boss of the class, approached and evaluated his work like an old man. "Ah yes, this is exquisite."

Everyone in the classroom burst into laughter at his usual antics.

One day, when the afternoon class started, everyone was

making a big fuss, instigated by Masato Tanaka and Hideo Kondo. Katsumasa Kawanakajima, who had a strong sense of justice, warned the two of them to hush, but they didn't listen. However, the teacher didn't seem to care at all, and started playing the tiny organ with all his might. It was a famous song that Naoto often heard, but couldn't name. When Naoto asked Toshihiro, the brightest in his class, the boy proudly replied, "This is a famous European song called 'Nobara', by Brendan Schubert of Austria. It's one of Goethe's poems set to music, a sad love song."

The teacher continued playing the organ until everyone was quiet, and then he began to cry sadly. As expected, the two bad boys were surprised enough to quiet down. Then the teacher started class as if nothing had happened. Naoto was deeply moved by the fact that Mr. Kuroiwa's teaching method of 'waiting quietly until everyone realizes what is wrong' was very different from the hysterical teacher at his old school.

One day, Mr. Kuroiwa suddenly asked Naoto, "What do you think of war?"

Naoto replied right away, "I hate war."

The teacher invited Naoto to the side, saying, "Okay, let's go somewhere together after class." However, the teacher also invited Tomiyan, Toshihiro, Tsuguo, and Fumiko. The teacher took five students, including Naoto, to the third floor of the Hamanomachi arcade. In the meeting room on the third floor, five or six middle-aged men who also looked like teachers were already sitting and waiting. As soon as everyone was gathered, the room darkened, and a large picture was projected on the screen. It was a tragic movie about the Vietnam War. In other words, it was the anti-war activity of the Japan Teachers' Union

The Vietnam War went into full swing in 1965, the year after the Tokyo Olympics, and continued for ten years. It ended with the fall of Saigon, the capital of Vietnam, which was divided into the socialist North Vietnam and capitalist South Vietnam. It became a proxy war between the two great powers, the Soviet Union and the United States. At this time, the United States tried to make amends in a quagmire of guerrilla warfare, using inhumane weapons, such as chemical defoliants and mass-killing napalm bombs. It was also known in Japan that conjoined twins named Beto and Doku were born due to the effects of chemicals.

Those acts, which can be called war crimes, had long haunted many Vietnamese people. It was exactly the same as the tragedy of World War II, in which more than 200,000 people were killed in an instant in Hiroshima and Nagasaki. There were still many survivors and second- and third-generation survivors who were suffering from the aftermath.

For some reason, the tragic slides of the Vietnam War that Naoto saw in that conference room seemed to overlap with the photos of the tragic victims he had seen at the Nagasaki Atomic

Bomb Museum. Both were victims of the United States.

However, it seems that few people criticized the United States, which dropped the atomic bombs. Rather, the majority of Japanese people worshiped and longed for the United States. At that time, the mindset of the Japanese people was, 'America is a splendid democratic country. Catch up and overtake America!'

The great thing about the United States of America was that it did not make the people of the defeated nations feel antipathy. Naoto at that time was no exception. To put it in extreme terms, it was like an infectious disease. He was fond of painting tanks and submarines back then, and he often drew them in his notebook. Naoto may have simply been fond of tanks and submarines, but he certainly had a longing for the United States.

Mr. Kuroiwa must have been a young anti-war member of the Japan Teachers' Union. If a school teacher were to take his students to an anti-war rally in modern days, he would surely be scolded by the board of education. But, it had been allowed at that time. However, because of this, Naoto became interested in anti-war activities, so Mr. Kuroiwa's influence was truly enormous. In his third year at university, Naoto was surprised by a feature article in a newspaper. It was an article about the people in Oak Ridge, Tennessee, who built the atomic bomb in the United States. "Oak Ridge residents still believe that the atomic bombs dropped on Hiroshima and Nagasaki were used to hasten the end of the war, and boast that they actually saved many Americans."

Did they really think like that? What did they think about the fact that the atomic bombings of Hiroshima and Nagasaki took the lives of more than 200,000 civilians, mainly women and children, in an instant? With the atomic bombs dropped only one week before the end of the war, could it really be said that they ended the war?

It was far more than a war crime that Japan was used as a nuclear test site by the United States for the first time in human history. Even today, the United States has not apologized to the survivors. Even in Japan, the only country to have suffered atomic bombings, not many people knew that the United States committed war crimes twice, in Japan and Vietnam.

It was said that history repeats itself, and Russian President Vladimir Putin was doing exactly the same thing as the United States–Russia's military invasion of Ukraine. Plus, in the near future, there was a high possibility that the same thing would be repeated on the Korean Peninsula and Taiwan.

Former Soviet Union President Gorbachev passed away on August 30th, 2022 at the age of 91. He won the Nobel Peace Prize for ending the Cold War as the first and last president of the Soviet Union. He was a true leader who contributed to world peace more than Kennedy and Obama in the United

States ever had. In fact, he had also visited Hiroshima and Nagasaki during his presidency. He must have learned so much about the tragedy of the atomic bomb, as he said, "I would like President Putin to follow suit, saying, "There is no other way to resolve disputes between countries other than dialogue."

History would prove whether he was a great leader or not. Gorbachev and Putin would likely be handed down as leaders who contrasted well in history. However, the evaluation of the two in Russia seems to be the complete opposite of how the world sees them. When asked who was the true leader, President Gorbachev, who led the former Soviet Union to its collapse, or President Putin, who is trying to restore the Soviet Union, no one outside of Russia would say Putin.

Chapter 4 Club Activities

On April 1st, 1965, the 6th grade class entered Nagasaki Municipal Umegasaki Junior High School (often nicknamed 'Umechu'). The school had opened in 1947, shortly after the war. In August of 1969, the year after Naoto and others graduated from the same school, a new school building made of reinforced concrete was completed. At that time, Umechu had 13 classes per grade, with about 45 students enrolled in each class, about 600 students in each grade, and 1,800 students in total. In modern day, the number of students enrolled is rapidly declining.

The main difference between elementary school and junior high school was 'club activities'. At the time, Naoto didn't have a clear goal of what kind of club he wanted to join. About a week after he entered the school, he considered the 'table tennis club', simply because he felt that he could do well at it.

Three of his other friends had already decided to join the table tennis club. So naturally Naoto did as well, but he regretted it immediately. Even in a casual school club, there was an extremely strict hierarchical system between each grade. It was not an atmosphere that did not allow anyone to speak up. Anyway, the first-years spent their days silently repeating practice swings.

Naoto asked Captain Motomura, a third-year student, a question. "I know that practice swings are the basis of table tennis, but I feel like just practicing swings like this every day for a year won't help us improve. Wouldn't match-style practice be more practical?"

"I know what you're trying to say," the older boy said. "You're probably sick of swinging. But first-year students don't touch the ping-pong ball for a year, they just stick to swinging. It's tradition, we can't change it now."

Naoto made up his mind that there would be no tomorrow for a table tennis club that could not improve on such irrational traditions, and left the club less than a month after joining. The table tennis club was later abolished, and another one never took its place. In order not to make the same mistake, Naoto visited various club activities to sample what they did. In the midst of this, he saw a student wearing a small pair of glasses writing something down in a notebook on their way to the gymnasium. Naoto followed out of curiosity, but he ended up running into the basketball club, who asked him to join.

"No, I'm just taking a look around."

"Well then stay and take a proper look," the older kid said and brought out a folding chair for Naoto. Before long, the other members of the basketball club finished their classes and gathered in groups of threes and fives to practice. The last person to appear was Mr. Shigemori, a social studies teacher who was also the adviser to the basketball club. The small boy from earlier handed a note to the teacher right away.

"Thank you, Mizutani." The adviser patted the smaller boy on the shoulder as he scurried back to the sidelines. The kid ended up being the manager of the basketball club, responsible for drafting a team list, and handing it over to the teacher.

The teacher gathered everyone and announced the starting line-up for today's match. The club members who weren't called didn't seem upset, satisfied with the proposed line-up by Manager Mizutani. Seeing this, Naoto thought that Manager Mizutani was highly trusted by both the club members and teachers. He later found out that Mizutani was a second-generation survivor of the atomic bombing and suffered from leukemia, making it impossible for him to exercise heavily. Naoto decided to join the basketball club, which was a stark contrast to the dark atmosphere of the table tennis club. At the time, the basketball club had 3 third-year students, 6 second-year students, and 9 first-year students, including Naoto, for a total of 18 members. The whole club had a free and open atmosphere that encouraged everyone to participate.

However, shortly after he joined the club, Naoto noticed something. Among the eight students other than Naoto, there were three top of their class geniuses on the team. Naoto did not rank within the top 100 in the exams held right after he entered junior high school. The three geniuses who did were Yuji Manda, Tatsunosuke Arie, and Hideo Iida, who were always in the top ten. Naoto never managed to outdo them during his freshman year.

Balancing literary and athletic skills seemed to be the tradition in Umechu's basketball club. However, during matches with other schools, they were a rather weak team that was never able to make it through the first round. Still, Mr. Shigemori, the advisor, did not care about their streak of losses. "It's okay to lose, just have fun! This isn't the big leagues."

And after they would lose a match, he would say, "This means there are plenty of possibilities for us to win from now on. Life is long!"

He commuted from the countryside of Shikimi to the school by bus, and still stayed to teach the club members until late after school. It was when Naoto returned to his hometown in 2004 for the Obon Festival that he found out his teacher had passed away at the age of eighty-six. The motto of Umechu's basketball team was, "Regardless of the result, value the process." The basketball club was one of the few club activities that remained in Umechu for both men and women.

One day when Naoto and the others were in their third year, the captain of the basketball club asked Naoto and the others for advice. The captain was a smart theorist and tactician. Even during basketball games, he could think of various formations and get them to the verge of winning. But they still could never make it through the first round. To do something about it, he wanted to ask the members of the volleyball club, who were always said to be the favorites to win. The top players from that team went home with them after school. Once everyone had gathered, the captain thanked everyone and immediately got to the point. "Our basketball club practices for two hours on weekdays and over five hours on weekends. I don't think there is that much of a difference between our practice time and the volleyball club's, but why are you guys called favorites for the championship? What's different about us?"

"Well, are you guys in the basketball club really practicing seriously? If you ask me, I don't think there's a policy in your practice."

When the captain heard that, he didn't quite understand what he was saying. "What do you mean by policy?"

"Your policy is a 'strategy'. In other words, it's the direction we should aim for in our club activities. What is your basketball club's strategy?"

The captain thought about that sudden question for a while. "Our strategy is to practice more than anyone else."

The volleyball captain sneered. "That isn't a strategy or anything. It's just trying to do your best with guts. Listen carefully. Strategy begins with identifying the weaknesses of your team. Then, think of an action plan on how to overcome those weaknesses. Specifically, our weakness in the volleyball club was, as you can see, our height is overwhelmingly shorter than other teams. In any ball game when the skill is even, the team with the tallest average height always wins. You guys in the basketball club probably have the same problem as us. Once the direction has been clarified, the next step is to decide what to do with the action plan."

The team's remarks were truly eye-opening for the basketball club members. They all decided there were three tactics. The first was simple, even if you were shorter than your opponent, if you broke them down with your first move, you could score points without letting them attack. Then they had to practice those moves in particular. The team continued that every day for three months.

The second strategy was proposed by the receiver, Hiroshi. "As a receiver, I spent three days without sleeping thinking about how I could beat my opponent. We all spent time practicing our spin receiving. In this way, we continue to pick up the ball in the rally against the opponent, and then wait for them to make a mistake."

The third tactic was a 'Feint Toss'. They pretended to attack and jumped while tossing the ball to Takeshi and Yoichiro. Then the opponent's block was completely out of range. These tactics had an unexpectedly large effect. Umechu's basketball club, which had always lost in the first round, was reborn as a strong team that made it into the top 8.

In the blink of an eye, the final club activities of his third year ended, and Naoto and the others graduated from Umechu. Though all of his basketball club friends joined the basketball club in high school as well. One day, when Naoto finished practice and looked out the window, he saw the rugby club members practicing on the ground covered in mud. Among them were the previous volleyball captains. It seems that the two did not rejoin.

One of them later answered, "Naoto, when we were in junior high school, we thought that volleyball was our reason for living. Little by little, the direction drifted, and the gap grew with time. It was beautiful back then, but it no longer connected. It got too lonely."

His close friends from those days were continuing their own successful lives as adults.

Chapter 5 Penpals

Naoto finished up his important role as secretary for the elementary school's first reunion in fifty years, and the tension he had been holding onto disappeared all at once. Once he got back to his old nursing care routine, he received a text message. The email was from Emily Takayama, who had come all the way from Fukuoka to attend the reunion the other day.

"Naoto," it read, "thank you for your hard work with the alumni association. I was wondering if you could create a group LINE for everyone. It's like exchanging emails, but faster and with everyone involved. I would love to have Naoto coordinate it."

He pondered for a while what the purpose of launching the group LINE was. If he limited it to close friends only, he could expect complaints from those who hadn't heard from anyone in a while. There was a possibility that people would complain. He decided to consult with Tomiyan, the chairman of the alumni association.

"Well, how about sending out an email saying anyone is free to join or decline? Let's leave the content of the emails up to everyone's common sense, let each person do their own thing."

Due to the chairman's decisiveness, the group LINE of classmates was set up. Naoto remembered everyone's mischievous behavior, and it didn't seem to change with age. One problem that did arise though was that half the members couldn't figure out how to use LINE on their smartphones. They ended up making a separate email chain for those without the app, but the emails Naoto sent were never marked as 'read'. In the end, out of the twelve members, only nine, excluding Naoto, always read the messages, through LINE or email.

In addition, Miho Kuroi withdrew from LINE partway through because the ring tone was too annoying. Ryoko Arai, Keiko Kabumori, Mieko Uchimata, and Takashi Miyata also chose to use individual emails over a group LINE. When Naoto opened the group LINE, he thought about how to provide common topics for everyone. Even family-to-family group LINEs often went unused over time. Therefore, in order to keep it going, he thought it would be important to keep discussing common topics of interest.

However, it turned out that his efforts weren't necessary. After starting the group LINE, everyone began to openly post their own principles and opinions, such as old memories, current hobbies, and various worries as elderly people. It was as if he was hearing the continuation of the class reunion the other day. Everyone's posts were read as soon as they were uploaded, and all were read within the same day. With this, the group LINE finally got on track, and Naoto was no longer needed to facilitate. He returned to a lonely and unpredictable life at home with no communication. During the past eight years of his life as a caregiver, in the beginning, he was nervous every day and had no time to feel stressed. But as time passed, he was able to see things that he had been unable to see because he was so absorbed in it. Before he knew it, the sickness of compiling stress was gnawing at Naoto's heart.

Naoto started volunteering, but it had since been suspended due to a cluster of COVID-19 outbreaks at the venue. At that time, the group LINE started up again, and as a result, Naoto's stress was gradually relieved. For Naoto, these virtual pen pals were a wonderful gift from the alumni association. There were seven years left until the next reunion, but the group LINE would hold everyone's hearts together until then.

"Good luck to everyone! Cheers to those days of our youth when we didn't have any worries! Let's meet again at the next class reunion! Until then, everyone stay healthy!"

Chapter 6 Family Collapse

The fierce battle over inheritance between Naoto's brother-in-law and sister-in-law began with the death of his mother-in-law on December 7th, 2019, and ended when his brother-in-law filed for the Fukuoka Family Court in Omuta in September 2020. Although the case was filed for 'arbitration' with the branch office and the case was tried for two years, the parties were unable to reach a settlement. During that time, at the request of his brother-in-law, Naoto provided full support, such as filing an application for arbitration, analyzing his mother-in-law's transactions with financial institutions, and writing a statement of opinion in response to his sister-in-law's complaint. However, the arbitration still ended in failure.

At one point, the 'inheritance division agreement' that Naoto proposed to arbitrate between the two was on the verge of agreement, but then his brother-in-law could not forgive his sister-in-law and went back to the drawing board. Naoto couldn't help but regret why the family, who had been on good terms until now, had to continue such miserable strife.

The brother-in-law withdrew the arbitration, and on March 18th, 2022, asked the Nagasaki Family Court to 'return the unjust enrichment' as he could not forgive the sister-in-law's misconduct.

The amount to be refunded was the tens of millions of yen that his sister-in-law had withdrawn from her mother-in-law's bankbook without permission when she was hospitalized due to dementia. It totaled about 20 million yen. Furthermore, in order to return the money, he seized the sister's bank account. However, the cash that she withdrew was used to pay off her husband's large debts, leaving her bankbook with only 100,000 yen left. Naoto asks the lawyer hired by his brother to investigate the past actions of his sister-in-law's deposits. When back-calculating from the amount of withholding tax (20% of the interest) that was recorded in the copy of the bank passbook, the average balance of his sister-in-law's savings account was over 3 million yen.

Over the past twenty years, nearly 80 million yen had been withdrawn from his mother-in-law's bank account. That included the proceeds from the sale of securities that she managed at a brokerage firm. Yoko's mother used to tell Yoko and Naoto, "The securities entrusted to Gekkou Securities will be inherited by Kayo (the sister), and the securities entrusted to Nonomura Securities will be inherited by Yoko." However, after she passed away, the balance certificate from Gekko Securities had zero, and Nonomura Securities had halved the entrusted amount. The proceeds from the sale of these securities were also used to repay Kayo's husband's debt.

The presiding judge accepted the plaintiff's claim as justified and ordered the financial institution to submit past transaction details. Then, the data of this financial institution was delivered to the lawyer requested by his brother. Lawyer Ataka hastily sent that data to Naoto for confirmation. "Yamamoto, I was finally able to obtain the data that proves Yoko's sister's wrongdoing. Surprisingly, she withdrew a total of nearly 100 million yen from the bank account. Most of it was for the repayment of a large amount of debt from her husband. It must have been withdrawn in order to appropriate it."

"Is that so? Now we can finally see the future of this trial. The 'return of unjust enrichment' and the 'inheritance dispute' can all be resolved at once."

However, the sister conspired with her husband to take advantage of Yoko, who was bedridden and had no cognitive function. The sister-in-law's counterargument was as follows,

"The money I withdrew was a fair reward for caring for our mother on my own. I borrowed it and she still hasn't paid it back."

It was a last-ditch effort of a groundless objection that the cash she withdrew was legitimate nursing care remuneration. Because Yoko borrowed the money to buy the house from their mother and hadn't returned it, it was considered unfair profit. Her intention was to say that Yoko had also received a fair amount of cash from their mother and that she too is entitled to inherit the property left. In an attempt to back up that claim of hers, she asked Omasu Hayata, who was a junior high classmate of Yoko, to lie in court.

Unbeknownst to them, Hayata had a crush on the sister in the past, so he jumped at the task without question and fell into the trap set by her. Until now, Naoto had tried not to get involved in the fight between the siblings, but he had reached the limit of his patience with the sister's treatment of Yoko. Naoto stood up to protect Yoko.

The sister had thought that the data of her wrongdoing was submitted to the court, was disadvantageous to her. So she asked her husband to make up with Naoto, and asked Naoto's eldest son to mediate. However, it was far too late for pathetic attempts at peace. One by one, Naoto denounced his sister-in-law's wrongdoings with irrefutable evidence. First, Naoto clarified at the trial that the written statement from Hayata at the request of the sister was a complete lie.

Thankfully, Naoto always kept detailed receipts and calendars– it was information that a third party could never know. In other words, it was made clear that the sister had asked the man to lie for her.

There was even a part in the 'record' that said Yoko had told Naoto, "You should pay back the 20 million yen you borrowed from my mother while she is still healthy." It was impossible, considering that Yoko had almost no cognitive function at that time. Naoto provided the presiding judge with documentary evidence to prove that the story from Omasu was a lie. Afterwards, Naoto expressed his opinion about the succession dispute so far.

"Presiding Judge, my name is Naoto Yamamoto, I am Yoko's husband. My wife is bedridden due to an intractable disease, so I would like to express my opinion as the adult guardian of my wife. Since my mother-in-law has passed, the fierce inheritance dispute between my sister-in-law and brother-in-law has continued for more than three years. During that time, my wife's symptoms continued to worsen, she became unable to speak, and finally she almost lost all of her cognitive function. Yet, her sister didn't care that Yoko was suffering from an intractable disease, and kept repeating her own selfish claims. I was very disappointed that we had to have such a bloody fight, so I tried my best to repair the relationship, but in the end, both of them were merciless towards me, an outsider. Since my mother-in-law, who passed away, had entrusted me with a will saying, "If anything happens, I'll leave it up to you," I tried to arbitrate many times. If my wife, who my mother-in-law trusted the most among the three heirs, was in good health, I don't think it would have turned into such a ridiculous dispute. This problem was caused mainly by Kayo's husband's huge amount of debt. It's destroying her family, and is about to destroy my brother-in-law's family too. If Kayo's husband hadn't had a huge gambling debt, this wouldn't have happened. My mother-in-law knew that this would happen, so she entrusted me. When my brother-in-law first had this problem, he called me almost every day. At first, I also thought that mediation would work, but the lack of documented evidence for inheritance disputes between close relatives proved to be an unimaginably difficult situation. My sister-in-law, who was driven to the edge of a cliff, turned her attention to Yoko, who has no cognitive function at all, so I decided to investigate the wrongs of my sister-in-law and her husband. There is only one truth. My mother-in-law's large amount of cash was gone, and the large amount of securities entrusted had decreased significantly. From the fact that the securities were canceled and reduced to zero, and the fact that the sister-in-law's husband was repaying a large amount of debt during that time, the evil deeds of the sister and her husband are clear. When I think about my mother-in-law's chagrin, I feel very sorry."

However, that time, the plaintiff believed Omasu's story and began to distrust Naoto. Finally, Naoto asked the presiding judge, "I have one request. It's related to the nature of the inheritance dispute in this case. It was a large amount of debt problems. Therefore, the cash that my sister-in-law withdrew was used to repay it. The status of repayment of a large amount of debt from personal rehabilitation (the debt bar drawing system) has been applied for. If we clarify the process from the beginning to the completion of payment, this issue could be resolved. I request the submission of these documents."

After two weeks, all those documents were ready. It became clear that the sister's large amount of debt, which amounted to tens of millions of yen, had suddenly decreased to several million yen. And the mother's deposit was withdrawn to match the repayment. It completely drove his sister-in-law and her husband into a corner, and after that they were in a daze no matter what the judge asked them. Even so, Suma's family was in a mess with a large amount of debt from the loan. He couldn't forgive the husband's sins. Yoko's mother would be mourning the tragedy of her own family from beyond the grave.

Chapter 7 Mother's Life

Naoto's mother, Aiko, was born in Yatsushiro City in Kumamoto Prefecture on September 1, 1924, and soon after moved to Kitakyushu City, where she lived with her family until she was twenty years old. After Aiko graduated from Wakamatsu Girls' High School, she worked at the Tobata branch of Mitsukoshi Bank.

On the other hand, his father, Masao, had worked as a welder at Mitsubishi Shipyards in Nagasaki, changed jobs to Yawata Steel Works at the age of 28, and was lodging near Aiko's house. They married in March, 1946. After that, they moved to Nagasaki and opened a barber shop in Dozamachi. The two were blessed with three children, including Naoto, and the barber shop was successful for many years. However, when his father was 58 years old, his health deteriorated and he was forced to close the business. For more than ten years after that, his father was hospitalized at the nearby Showakai Hospital, and his mother went to the hospital every day to take care of him

After Masao passed away in May 2005, his mother spent the rest of her life happily enjoying her hobbies, Japanese dance, and shamisen. Every time Naoto returned to Nagasaki on a business trip, he saw his aging mother and had an idea–to teach her, who was interested in everything and had a strong love for learning, how to utilize her cellphone. His eldest daughter, Kumi, bought a large-screen phone for elderly people, and Naoto taught his 88-year-old mother how to use it. Just as Naoto expected, his mother picked up on it quickly.

She started sending text messages to Naoto almost every day. When Naoto was too busy to reply, she would call him and ask, "Didn't you receive my email?"

Shortly after that, Aiko developed Alzheimer's disease and she often wandered around in the middle of the night. So Naoto decided to take her to Kawasaki to live with him. However, around that time, Yoko's illness began to progress as well, so his mother wanted to reduce Naoto's burden. She said that she'd move into a paid nursing home in Tama Plaza. It was a newly built facility, just opened in March 2014, and was about to start recruiting residents. She was given a room on the second floor, near the elevator. Every Saturday or Sunday, Naoto always brought sweets and fruits when he came to visit. His mother loved sweets, and she would often tell Naoto that she wanted to eat red bean buns. His mother's peaceful life lasted for nearly two years. However, Yoko's illness continued to worsen during that time, and she began to self-harm frequently. Naoto was forced to make the difficult decision to take Yoko back to Nagasaki while leaving his mother with dementia in Kawasaki.

On July 22nd, 2016, Naoto decided to return to Nagasaki with Yoko and their dog Great. As a result, Naoto decided to ask his eldest daughter, Kumi, who lived in Zushi, to look after her grandmother. Naoto's cell was overloaded with calls from both the roadside station hospital in Nagasaki where Yoko was hospitalized and the nursing home in Yokohama where his mother was living. Naoto was in Nagasaki for Yoko's medical treatment at that time, so every time his phone rang, he prayed it was good news from the hospital. However, about every one out of three times, it was a call from a nursing home in Yokohama.

"Hello, this is Kuroda, I work at the nursing home in Tama Plaza where your mother resides. I'm sorry to say, but last night your mother was wandering the halls late at night and fell down from the stairs. The doctor came immediately and did a checkup. There were no particular abnormalities, but it's possible that she hit her head, so she went to the general hospital just in case. I am contacting you for consent forms."

Naoto immediately contacted Kumi, who had her grandmother taken to Yokohama General Hospital. Luckily, there were no particular problems.

However, one day, less than three months later, he received another phone call from the nursing home.

"Mr. Yamamoto, your mother has had a high fever since

last night, so she was examined by a visiting doctor. She said that your mother should immediately undergo a thorough examination at the hospital in Yokohama. I told her that you were in Nagasaki, but…"

"I understand. I think I can be there by tomorrow afternoon. Until then, thank you."

As a result of a detailed examination at Yokohama General Hospital, the fever turned out to be a kidney stone, but his mother would not be able to withstand surgery at 91 years old. Instead she was treated with medicine to hopefully disperse the stone. The next day, the doctor contacted Naoto. "Mr. Yamamoto, I have good news. Your mother's kidney stones have disappeared faster than expected. The fever should go away now. If things are going well, I think she will be able to leave the hospital next week."

"That was a big help. Thank you very much, doctor."

After that, Aiko didn't have any major illnesses for about three years, but her physical strength continued to decline due to old age.

About two months later, one morning, he received a phone call from Kumi. "Grandma was just urgently hospitalized at Shin-Yurigaoka General Hospital in Kawasaki with aspiration pneumonia."

"Okay. I'll be over there this evening. I'm sorry, but until then, watch over her for me."

In this way, Naoto was able to visit his mother a few days before she died. After that, he returned to Nagasaki, so unfortunately he could not see her in her final moments. Naoto was told by her doctor that she would not die any time soon, and to return to Nagasaki for the time being. Kumi was silent, only faintly crying on the other side of her phone–that's how Naoto found out she had died.

The next day, Kumi and his second son Tsubame cremated Aiko the same day and brought her remains back to Nagasaki. It was two months later when she was buried in the same grave as his father. Masao had waited seventeen years for Aiko.

The night of the service, Naoto had a dream that he and his mother were on a plane to Nagasaki. Aiko, perhaps because of her dementia, kept repeating the same thing to Naoto every time. "Actually, when I was in girls' school, there was a man I promised to marry in the future. My mother believed that I would definitely marry him. However, during the war, your father enthusiastically came to our house and protected us. I gave in to his enthusiasm and finally married your father."

When Naoto heard her story, he thought, "If she had married that man, I wouldn't have been born," and had mixed feelings in his dream. Naoto had thought that his mother had married his father from the beginning because she liked him, but for some reason in his dream he realized that his mother had a certain youthful charm about her when she spoke about

Masao. Considering Aiko's various hardships since then, he couldn't ask if it was really good for her to marry his father. His mother's life had never been smooth sailing. There was no doubt that it was full of ups and downs, but a full life nonetheless.

Chapter 8 Atomic Bomb Deadly Sin

At the end of the Pacific War, at 8:15 in the morning on August 6th, 1945, in Hiroshima, and three days later, at 11:02 in the morning of August 9th, in Nagasaki, the United States of America dropped an atomic bomb for the first time in human history. More than 100,000 people in Hiroshima and 74,000 people in Nagasaki lost their lives in a single instant. Those atomic bombings were widespread, indiscriminate, and inhumane, prohibited by international law, and were clearly war crimes. In the wake of Russia's military invasion of Ukraine on February 24th, 2022, Russian President Vladimir Putin said, "We will not hesitate to use nuclear weapons against any country that threatens Russia."

President Biden of the United States strongly condemned that statement, but it was none other than the United States that used Hiroshima and Nagasaki as a nuclear test site 77 years ago. The plutonium atomic bomb codenamed 'Fat Man' dropped on Nagasaki was said to have been 1.5 times more powerful than the uranium atomic bomb 'Little Boy' dropped on Hiroshima. However, since Nagasaki City was surrounded by mountains, the heat rays and blast were cut off, resulting in less damage than Hiroshima. The initial target of the atomic bomb dropped on Nagasaki was said to be Kokura. However, due to bad weather over Kokura (one theory is that there was a smoke screen), the astronauts were unable to visually confirm the city. Therefore, it was dropped on Nagasaki, which was the second target.

The atomic bomb was dropped 500 meters above Matsuyama Town in Nagasaki and devastated an area with a radius of about 1 kilometer in just a few seconds. The hypocenter was more than 3 kilometers away from the center of Nagasaki City and was surrounded by many mountains, including Mt. Konpira. However, Masao, who had temporarily returned from Shanghai, rushed to the epicenter of the explosion, with relief workers from the Oura area on the night of, and was exposed to secondary radiation. When the bomb hit, Suma was on a streetcar in front of Suwa Shrine, near the hypocenter. Luckily, Suma was on the train, so she didn't get directly hit by the blast and survived. If both of them had lost their lives in this terrible bombing, neither Naoto nor Yoko would have been born into the world.

Masao told Naoto, who had just entered junior high school, about that day. "Because I served in Shanghai for a long time as an interpreter, I returned to Japan before the end of the war and lived with my adoptive mother Kame in Oura Higashimachi. It was late at night by the time I was able to rush to Urakami, where the atomic bomb had been dropped, with a large cart. It was sweltering that day, and the temperature didn't drop even at night. Soon black rain began to fall. Countless men and women with their skin peeling and hanging off their bodies cried out, 'Give me water, please, water!' I couldn't help but look up at the sky above Mt. Konpira in the distance. I saw countless small fireballs flying around in the air. Probably, the souls of all the children who died instantly from the hot air that reached over 4000 degrees in mere seconds, wandering around without knowing what had happened to them. I couldn't help but burst into tears when I thought that those children still wanted to play in this world."

Masao and the rescue workers had carried the still-living A-bomb survivors to a facility with doctors and nurses, and then carried even more dead bodies to a makeshift crematorium. On the other hand, Suma, who was exposed to the atomic bombing in front of Suwa Shrine, thought she was only slightly injured at the time and counted her blessings. However, a terrible thing happened when her eldest daughter, Kumi, was born a year and a half later. It was the aftereffects of the atomic bomb. The tragedy of Suma's family started from there.

Seventy-two years later, the tragedy of an intractable disease was still affecting Yoko. Yoko made her sixth suicide attempt on August 8th, 2017, the day before thee 72nd Nagasaki Atomic Bomb Anniversary. She was discovered cutting her wrists by a neighbor in front of the houses that stood above

Glover Garden. An ambulance arrived immediately and she was taken to a public hospital.

Naoto had asked the Oura Police Station to search for Yoko, who had gone missing, so the police station contacted him as soon as she was found. Fortunately, the wound on Yoko's wrist was minor, so she healed fine. Naoto rushed to various psychiatric hospitals, but none of them would accept patients like Yoko who repeatedly self-harmed. He was at a loss and visited the consultation desk for mental disorders at Nagasaki City Hall. There, he was finally introduced to a psychiatric clinic, and, desperately, he asked the director to find a hospital where she could be admitted. However, it was difficult to find a hospital that would accept Yoko right away.

Meanwhile, Naoto received a phone call from Yoko's older sister in Omuta. "I asked the director of the Psychiatric Hospital about where Yoko should be hospitalized, so please go see him tomorrow at 2 o'clock. He knows about your situation well, so I think he'll accept you."

The next day, Naoto took Yoko to the bus bound for the hospital. The day was extremely hot, and Yoko, who was sensitive to heat, quickly became exhausted. She sat down on the bench at the bus stop, unable to take another step. Naoto somehow managed to coax her into getting on the bus, but he misread the schedule and got off the bus just before their destination. He stumbled with Yoko up the hill for fifteen minutes and at last she reached Hirota Psychiatric Hospital.

The inside of the hospital was strangely dim, even though it was daytime. They were immediately ushered into the interview room. Naoto fanned Yoko with her fan, but Yoko was breathing heavily through her mouth and seemed to be in pain. After a while, the director entered the interview room.

"That's right. It's been less than two months since we came back to Nagasaki, but she's had two incidents of self-harm. It happened four times when we were in Kawasaki, so six times total in eight months."

"I'm sorry, sir, but we cannot accept patients who self-harm. If we accept a patient in this kind of situation when there is a shortage of nurses, the entire hospital would stop working."

Naoto was at a loss. Finally, he went to ask the director of Tsukimachi Clinic, who was recommended by city hall. If it didn't work, he didn't know what to do. When the director saw Naoto's distressed state, he immediately set up an appointment for Yoko to be admitted to the hospital next week. The only condition was that Yoko would have to be restrained. It would be the second time been restrained while hospitalized. The first time was when she repeatedly self-harmed at their home in Kawasaki.

It seemed that Yoko's older sister, Kumi, also had to be put in that kind of condition. Kumi was born on February 10th, 1947, and died at Hirota Hospital in 1971, at the young age of

24. Then, at Kumi's 50th anniversary memorial service, Naoto's brother-in-law revealed something surprising to him. "Actually, Kumi had atomic-bomb hydrocephalus. When she was 20 years old, she developed a brain disorder and was admitted to Tagami Hirota Psychiatric Hospital, where she died four years later. The first symptom was losing her ability to walk, and then her cognitive function began to decline. Our mother was teaching a dressmaking class at the time, so we had no choice but to put Kumi in the hospital, because she couldn't take care of my sister all day. My sister was physically restrained to prevent her from falling, and it seems that her mental state gradually grew more unstable. At that time, the Japanese government was promoting forced sterilization for disabled people under the Eugenic Protection Law enacted after the defeat in the war. However, one day, she wasn't physically restrained, so she fell and hit her head, resulting in a fatal injury. It's impossible for us to know what happened at that time, but I can't help feeling that the hospital is hiding the truth. I wonder if Director Hirota knew something."

○ Atomic bomb hydrocephalus is a disease that causes abnormalities in the brain due to exposure to radiation from the atomic bomb. Abnormalities in the production, circulation, or absorption of cerebrospinal fluid cause cerebrospinal fluid to accumulate in the cranial cavity, causing the ventricles to become larger than normal.

Compression of the brain by cerebrospinal fluid then affects brain function, and the skull swells due to the pressure. Other symptoms are headache, vomiting, abnormal vision, blindness etc.

○ The Eugenic Protection Law was a law enacted after the war (1948) to restrict the birth of children by persons with disabilities. In the 48 years up to 1996 when it was repealed, 845,000 sterilization operations were performed.

While listening to his brother-in-law, Naoto realized something. The symptoms of his sister-in-law Kumi's atomic bomb hydrocephalus were very similar to those of Yoko. In both cases, the cause was the onset of abnormalities in the brain, and the speed at which it progressed was also the same. Both of their functions of the frontal lobe, which controls the ability to make decisions, had declined rapidly.

"Perhaps Yoko's illness is the same as her sisters'?"

If so, Yoko's illness may have been caused by her parent's exposure to the atomic bomb. Seventy-seven years after the atomic bombing, he was reminded once again of the terror of nuclear weapons, which continued to inflict aftereffects on survivors and their families.

Naoto's anger welled up.

"In any war, each side always has its own sense of justice, and it's difficult to decide which side is better or worse. If a solution cannot be reached through negotiation, the war will proceed, and both parties will have irreversible damage. There is no denying the possibility that the earth will be destroyed if a single mistake is made. In other words, there are no winners or losers in war. Only the weak, the elderly, women, and children lost."

In addition, President Putin's statement that he would 'not hesitate to use nuclear weapons' in the recent military invasion of Ukraine proves that the concept of 'nuclear deterrence' had become obsolete. It had also become apparent that even the coalition could not deter war. The possibility of war had increased dramatically.

It was the leader of the country who decided whether to start a war or not. As the only country in the history of humankind to have suffered atomic bombings, the compassionate leaders of Japan should now play a role in persuading the leaders of the countries in conflict to end the war. Only Japan can do that.

At least, the two splendid leaders who visited the atomic bombed cities of Japan during their presidency, conveyed the tragedy of atomic bombs to their home countries, and tried to eliminate nuclear weapons. He hoped that such a competent leader would appear in Japan as soon as possible. Before the earth is destroyed by incompetent leaders, Japan needs to also have a strong leader who can address the true horror of the atomic bomb to the world in their own words, and never repeat the tragedy of Kumi and Yoko.

Chapter 9 Father's Soul

Naoto's father, Masao Yamamoto, was born on March 1st, 1915 in the remote countryside of what is now Omuta City, Fukuoka Prefecture. He was the second son of his father, Ryuuichi, and his mother, Tsuki. However, the following year, on May 9th, 1916, he was adopted by Kame Yamamoto, who ran an okiya (a house where geisha and prostitutes are sent to meet requests from customers) in the entertainment district of Maruyama, Nagasaki.

Until he reached adulthood, Masao worked as a welder at Mitsubishi Shipyards in Nagasaki. During the Pacific War, he served in the navy in Shanghai, China, then returned to live with Kame in Oura Higashimachi. After that, he worked at Yawata Steel Works in present-day Kitakyushu City.

In Wakamatsu, where he was lodging, he met Aiko, who would become Naoto's mother, and they got married soon after. They then returned to Nagasaki, where he obtained a barber's license and opened the 'Yamamoto Barber Shop' on Harusame-dori in Dozamachi. However, Masao later developed a cerebral infarction and was forced to close the barber shop. It wasn't until Naoto began caring for Yoko that he understood the hardships of his mother, who had been caring for his father for so many years. His father suffered from a cerebral infarction, prostatic hyperplasia, and dementia, and in his later years was completely bedridden. Aiko said that every time she received a phone call from Showakai Hospital where Masao was hospitalized, she would think, "Is this finally the end?" His father truly passed away at the age of 89 on May 25th, 2005.

At that time, Naoto was the deputy director of the planning department at Tokyo Marunouchi Bank. On that day, he accompanied the president to the Bank of Japan Press Club in Nihonbashi to announce the financial results for the fiscal year of 2004. The night before, his mother had informed him that his father was in a critical condition, so when he heard the news of his death, he wasn't too surprised. He returned to Nagasaki first thing the next morning and went straight from Omura Airport to the funeral hall. At the funeral, more than 100 people attended. His eldest daughter, Kumi, who lived at Junshin High School in Nagasaki, also left classes early to attend.

After the funeral, Kumi went back to her high school student dormitory called Bethany Hall, but she found a newborn black Labrador puppy at a pet shop on the way. About a month later, she happened to pass by the same pet shop on her way home from her club's archery match. It seemed that the black Labrador puppy was staring at her. Kumi instinctively ran to the puppy and called out to him, practicing her English, "Hey, great!"

The puppy lifted her head like she was being called, and barked at Kumi. After that, the puppy would really be called 'Great'. A few days later, Kumi called Naoto in Kawasaki.

"Hello, Dad? Hey, could I keep a black Labrador, her name is 'Great'?"

Kumi rarely asked for anything, so Naoto immediately agreed to her unusual request, and agreed to keep 'Great' in Kawasaki while she was at boarding school. Yoko picked up the dog from Nagasaki on Saturdays and Sundays and brought her home in Kawasaki.

Great became part of the family from that day on, along with their golden retriever, Aki. Great was happy to see Aki and wagged her tail as if the other dog was her own mother. However, a few days later in the morning, Naoto forgot to take his arrhythmia pill, which he was supposed to take every morning, and went to work. As soon as he arrived at his office, he got a call from Yoko. Naoto had a bad feeling because Yoko rarely called him at his work number.

"Hello, honey? Great is acting strangely. She seems to be having trouble breathing and is occasionally groaning and having convulsions. I'm thinking of taking her to a veterinarian, but...do you have any idea why this happened?"

After thinking about it for a while, Naoto suddenly shouted, "That's right. I forgot to take my heart medicine and I left next to the window this morning. Is it still there?"

"No, it's not. Naoto, do you think Great ate the medicine?"

"It's likely. Anyway, take her to the vet as soon as possible and tell the doctor that she may have accidentally ingested Rythmodan. If a dog takes human medicine, it's going to be terrible."

Thus, Great was admitted to the animal hospital. They didn't tell Kumi about it. Their two sons, who lived nearby in Tokyo, were worried about Great and came to visit. About a week later, on the night of July 12th, Great left for heaven without ever waking up. Naoto regretted his carelessness and Yoko regretted letting Great into their house in the first place. The Great was cremated at noon the next day.

Yoko said to Naoto, "I can't bear to tell Kumi that Great passed away. Let's go to a pet shop and look for an identical black Labrador."

They looked around several pet shops and finally found a black Labrador puppy that looked a lot like Great. It was slightly smaller, but they decided to keep the puppy, knowing that it would be bigger by the time Kumi graduated from Junshin High School in Nagasaki and returned to Kawasaki next March. They thought everything would be fine, but when Kumi came back after graduating and saw this new Great, she said, "Great's nose looks bigger. I feel like it's somehow different."

Yoko watched from behind with a worried look on her face. "That's not true. Her nose was big from the beginning."

They weren't sure if Kumi was convinced, but she didn't pursue it further.

Naoto remembered when Great died, and noticed something strange. First, Kumi happened to find the puppy near the funeral home where he held his father's funeral. And when Naoto met the second Great, he felt like the dog was staring at him from afar. Naoto searched for the papers from the pet shop to confirm something. The certificate had the date and time of Great's birth on it–May 25th, 2005 at 4:30 in the afternoon. Naoto got goosebumps when he saw that. It was the same day that his father died, and even the time was the same. He remembered because the financial results were announced at that time, and Naoto received the news of his father's death around the time the Bank of Japan Press Club announced its financial results.

Naoto also noticed something even more surprising. The first Great passed away on July 12th, 2005. Counting from May 25, 2005, when his father passed away, it was exactly 49 days. The 49th day after death was the day that the soul of the deceased departed from this world to the other world. Naoto could hardly believe that those things were mere coincidences.

During the 49 days that his father's soul remained in this world, he believed that he possessed the body of the first Great and came in order to bid farewell to Naoto's family.

His death had been sudden, but inevitable–none of Naoto's family had been around his deathbed at the time. His father had been put up for adoption as soon as he was born, he was never raised by his biological parents, and he was left unattended when he died. He probably wasn't the kind of father who would care about such sentimental things, but at the end of his life, there must have been something he wanted to tell Naoto. Great, possessed by his father's soul, may have tried to teach Naoto how strong his heart medicine was. Afterwards, Naoto asked the doctor in charge of the clinic whether he should continue to take that pill, and the doctor replied, "This is a pretty strong drug, so I'm more worried about the side effects. Your arrhythmia has subsided, so it might be time to stop taking it."

If it weren't for Great accidentally taking the pill, Naoto might have continued to take this drug. Ever since he was born, Naoto had no memories of playing with his father or going on trips. His only memory of his father was him always at work or having a drink after work while watching his children. His father's life may have been lonely from his birth until his death, but his only happiness would have been that he married his mother and was blessed with three children. His life was devoted to work, and it may have been a modest life, but he always looked forward to having a drink at night around his family.

Afterwards, Naoto visited his father's grave. "Dad, thank you for protecting my family for so long. I hope that I will be born as your child again in the next life."

Epilogue To the Distant World

Naoto's routine was to get up at four every morning, starting the day by putting on a CD of Yoko's favorite music. He leaves the music on until she goes to bed at night. Since taking care of her at home, he had bought more than fifty of these CDs. The first CD was all of her nostalgic folk songs that was lent to them by their dog park friend, Mrs. Onoyama. Yoko had probably heard the music thousands of times before.

When she started home care, she could still move her mouth slightly to the songs, but lately she'd grown completely unresponsive. Her recent check-up showed that the frontal lobe of her brain was far more atrophied than the last time. Yoko's cognitive function seemed to be almost gone, and she may not have even been able to recognize music.

Naoto then brushes her teeth, sucks out mucus from her airway, and disimpacts her bowels. He then does her in-bed stretching and massages her limbs, followed by a diaper change. If he ever neglected the massage, her limbs would stiffen and he wouldn't be able to change her diapers at all. This was all first thing in the morning.

After that, it took about two hours to administer nutrition through her gastrostomy port and then give her all her medicine.

Then the mucus generated by the nutrition administration through the gastrostomy needed to be sucked out again. Finally the nursing care for the morning would finally be completed. However, the routine was done four times a day, morning, afternoon, evening, and right before going to bed.

After Yoko had gone to sleep, Naoto's day would finally begin. His free time was about three hours from 9 to 12 at night. At that time, he does chores, such as writing down the details of her care for that day, preparing for the next day, watching the news, doing some muscle exercises, and preparing documents to be submitted to various courts and government offices.

About an hour before he goes to bed, he writes out his own history to prepare for the end of his life, which he started two years prior. It is his long-cherished desire to be able to close the curtain on his life while rereading said history.

It would soon be three years since they returned to Kawasaki and started home care. Yoko's illness began around 2014, so her period of assistance and care was about to reach ten years. When she underwent her second thorough examination at Tozai Hospital in Nagasaki, Dr. Asai told them that Yoko's illness was progressing. He had said that the average life expectancy would be five to seven years after the onset of supranuclear palsy, but Yoko has already surpassed that.

Naoto often thought about what would happen in the future, but he always stopped thinking about it halfway through and said to himself, "Whatever will be, will be."

But maybe it was time for him to take it seriously.

Both Naoto and Yoko would turn 70 the following February. The life left for both of them wouldn't be that long. In ten years, Naoto's sons would be in their early fifties, and his eldest daughter in her mid-forties. It was time for them to prepare their children for their passing.

The day prior, Naoto had a dream in which his family gathered around to discuss it. "It's about time I need to tell everyone. The two of us are already 70 years old. There was no doubt that their parents would pass away before them. When that time would come, he wanted to tell everyone in advance what to expect. If Yoko passed away first, there might not be a problem, but if Naoto passed first, there would be a huge decision. The children would have to choose whether to take care of their mother at home or to put her in the hospital.

Up until then, Naoto had managed to deal with their mother's health by providing in-home nursing care, but he had also spent a long time learning a great deal about how hospitals deal with patients like Yoko who were unable to communicate. Due to the lack of manpower at the hospital, it was absolutely impossible to provide constant nursing care.

They all had a conversation about it. "By the way, who would take care of your mother if I weren't around?"

The first to speak was Shota, the eldest son. "I'll take care of her. However, the house we live in now is pretty small, so it'd be difficult to care for her there." Shota's oldest child was in his early twenties, his second son, Ryo, was in high school, his daughter Mei was in middle school, and his youngest son was in elementary school. So, there would be plenty of people in their home for a long time.

Naoto and Yoko's second son, Tsubame, was dependent on his older brother and sister.

And finally, their eldest daughter, Kumi, gave her opinion, just as Naoto had thought. "I fought with mom and ran away from home. So if something happens to you, I would take care of her to make up for those lost years."

Each of their answers were almost exactly what Naoto had expected. The conclusion ended on Shota getting a larger home when the time came. Naoto woke up right as they decided.

The other decision was trying to imagine what Yoko thought about their situation. Naoto had thought about this question many times before, but he still hadn't found the answer. When Yoko had been in good health, she would often declare in front of everyone, "I definitely don't want to take life-prolonging measures. If I'm gone, pull the plug."

However, those had been Yoko's thoughts when she was healthy, and he had no idea what Yoko was thinking now. Dr. Asai had said that Yoko's life expectancy was five to seven years–but that seemed to only be the case for patients in the hospital, where it was difficult to provide sufficient nursing care and clear airways in the middle of the night due to the lack of manpower. Therefore, there were many cases of death due to aspiration pneumonia in hospitals. Since he could provide detailed care at home one-on-one, the risk of dying from aspiration pneumonia was far lower.

But if Yoko no longer had the will to live in her current state, the in-home nursing care might be something that went against her will. If Yoko was happy now and wanted to live longer, Naoto would be happy to continue taking care of her diligently. However, as Yoko kept her eyes closed all day, she couldn't even recognize who Naoto was. One hot day in August, Naoto woke up in the middle of the night because it was too hot and humid. Yoko was also drenched in sweat. He hurriedly turned on the air conditioner, changed Yoko's clothes, and washed them both off. When he was about to go back to sleep, something white was floating around Yoko sleeping on her bed. When Naoto rushed over, it disappeared. Naoto cried out involuntarily, "What? What was that just now!"

In her bed, Yoko was sound asleep as if nothing had happened. As usual, Naoto put his hand on Yoko's forehead to check if she had a fever.

The next morning, Naoto woke up at 4 o'clock in the morning as usual and thought about the previous night. When he looked out the window, it was still dark, but that white thing was still floating around the balcony of the third floor. Gradually, it began to look like a person, albeit vaguely. When Naoto approached the veranda, there were two figures staring into the inside of the house. Upon closer inspection, they looked like Yoko's mother, Suma, and her older sister, Kumi. Naoto hesitantly went out onto the balcony. Then, once again, the two of them suddenly disappeared. When he whipped his head around, the two of them were looking at Yoko sleeping on the bed, trying to hug her.

At that time, Yoko opened her eyes by herself and said to Naoto, "Thank you, Naoto."

It sounded like Yoko's final goodbye. For the bright and active Yoko, it must have been a long and boring bedridden life. Thinking about it, Yoko had worked hard for a long time. At that time, Naoto could see the faces of many people who had helped him in various aspects of his life–childhood friends from kindergarten and elementary school, friends from college, colleagues and bosses from his banking days, and the many people in the medical and nursing care fields.

Tears welled up in his eyes. "Thank you so much for your help over the years."

One day, Naoto had a dream about Yoko. It was a dream where he put Yoko in her wheelchair and they went to watch a beautiful sunset over the sea of Nagasaki.

Yoko smiled happily at her husband and said, "Naoto,

thank you so much for your time. May your future be even a hundred times happier!"

Postscript

He started writing this series when Yoko was hospitalized for the first time in a psychiatric hospital in Nagasaki, and Naoto kept a detailed record of her nursing care every day to check the effects of the medicine that had been administered to her. Once he started writing, he couldn't stop. Amidst the spread of the new coronavirus infection, he wanted to let his children know how their parents were doing, even while separated by quarantine. He wanted to tell his children, who grew up in a family-like environment, all about his own life up to this point, so he decided to compile a personal history as well.

At first, he intended to stop with just one book, but he couldn't finish it with just that.

After that, he compiled the second volume. Meanwhile, Yoko's condition progressed relentlessly until she had almost no cognitive function and no longer knew who her husband, Naoto, was.

Ten years had passed since Naoto began caring for Yoko in a desperate attempt to heal her, and before he knew it, both of them had reached the age of 70. So, Naoto started writing this third volume as the final chapter, hoping that it would help them both to finish their lives.

The biggest common theme throughout the trilogy is 'repaying the favor' to the many people who have helped them in various aspects of their lives. The 'Bank Edition' was the story of Naoto's career, the 'Education Edition' was an episode of struggling at his second workplace after retiring from the bank, the 'Nursing Edition' was Yoko's fierce battle against illness, and the 'Family Edition' was the story of the destiny of each family who raised them. The last addition, 'Nostalgia', begins with Naoto's childhood memories, reminiscing about his wonderful youth when he was a student and when he was a new employee.

As he was writing the final part, he learned that Yoko's older sister had passed away from complications of atomic bomb hydrocephalus. Naoto was astonished to learn that the tragedy of the atomic bombing of Nagasaki might have also affected Yoko's intractable disease. He continued to pursue what society should aim for in the future for socially vulnerable people.

He also realized that 'family love' was the common theme through every part of his writing. The subtitle of the final volume, 'Towards a Distant World', expresses a world in which Naoto and Yoko try to live through the past and present to the fullest, and live with hope in their hearts toward the 'future' that is about to come. As it is said that 'life is a drama without a plot', the lives of the two of them came to an unexpected twilight. They were overwhelmed by various difficult problems in Yoko's daily home-nursing care, and there were many times when Naoto almost gave up. Also, more than once, he prayed that god would come and carry Yoko, who was suffering from an intractable disease, as soon as possible. However, it was the familial love that made him reconsider fulfilling their natural lifespan until the very end.

The two of them were about to start walking towards the next world, the 'future'. The two, who were born and raised in Nagasaki, looked back on their lives while gazing at the sun setting over the beautiful Nagasaki sea, and looked forward to their future, in a distant world.

This work is a novel based on the author's own life, but the events also include fiction. Personal names and company names are pseudonyms and have nothing to do with any real-life counterparts.

About the author

Katsumi Yamaguchi

Born in Nagasaki Prefecture in 1953, he is a graduate of Nagasaki University. He joined a major metropolitan bank in 1976, and after working at the Fukuoka branch and the Motosumiyoshi branch, he was transferred to the Planning Department of the bank for a quarter of a century. During that time, he served under eight different presidents, liberalized interest rates, helped end the convoy system, listed on the New York Stock Exchange, BIS capital ratio regulation, financial big bang, bubble burst, bad debt problem, FSA inspection, bank collapse, management Experience the turbulent period of banks such as integration and Lehman shock. After he retired from the bank, he was the secretary general of the Accounting Education Foundation, and he focused on rebuilding the foundation, promoting accounting education, and fostering younger generations. He then devoted himself to home care to care for his wife, who suffered from his intractable disease.

著者プロフィール

山口 勝美 (やまぐち かつみ)

1953年長崎県生まれ。長崎大学卒。1976年に大手都市銀行に入行し福岡支店、元住吉支店を経て四半世紀にわたり、同行企画部に在籍。その間、八人の頭取に仕え、金利の自由化、護送船団方式の終焉、ニューヨーク証券取引所上場、BIS自己資本比率規制、金融ビッグバン、バブル崩壊、不良債権問題、金融庁検査、銀行破綻、経営統合、リーマンショックなどまさに銀行の激動期を身をもって体験。銀行退職後は教育財団の事務局長として、財団の再建、会計教育および後進の育成に注力した。その後、難病に罹った妻を介護するため、在宅介護に専念。

翻訳者プロフィール

Harley Emmons (ハーレイ エモンス)

(Japanease to English Translation & Localization)
I have done freelance work for various companies, such as Amazon, Honda, Mizuho Bank, and numerous medical suppliers and IT companies, for over six years.

Giving Back One-Hundred-Fold Volume3

Departure To the Distant World （人生の百倍返し　英訳版3）

2023年9月15日　初版第1刷発行

著　者　YAMAGUCHI Katsumi
発行者　瓜谷 綱延
発行所　株式会社文芸社
　　　　〒160-0022 東京都新宿区新宿1－10－1
　　　　　　　　電話 03-5369-3060（代表）
　　　　　　　　03-5369-2299（販売）

印刷所　株式会社晃陽社